SYSTEMA PARADOXA

ACCOUNTS OF CRYPTOZOOLOGICAL IMPORT

VOLUME 04
ALL-THE-WAY HOUSE
A TALE OF THE JERSEY DEVIL

AS ACCOUNTED BY KEITH R.A. DECANDIDO

NEOPARADOXA

Pennsville, NJ

2021

PUBLISHED BY
NeoParadoxa
A division of eSpec Books
PO Box 242
Pennsville, NJ 08070
www.especbooks.com

ISBN: 978-1-949691-71-9
ISBN (ebook): 978-1-949691-70-2

Interior Design: Danielle McPhail
www.sidhenadaire.com

Cover Art: Jason Whitley
Cover Design: Mike and Danielle McPhail, McP Digital Graphics
Interior Illustration: Jason Whitley

Copyediting: Greg Schauer and John L. French

Dedication

For ToniAnn, my favorite Jersey Devil

Chapter One

Atlantic City
State of New Jersey, United States of America
February 2020

"Why are we even *coming* to the office? It's *freezing*."

Valentina Perrone smiled at the plaintive wail of her apprentice. She was trying to find the right keys to her storefront office on the corner of Atlantic Avenue and North Carolina Avenue. Her leather gloves made that search take a bit longer, which was probably why Sarah el-Guindi was standing behind her complaining and shivering.

Finally locating the right ones, she unlocked the padlock that kept the bolt in place. With the lock off, the bolt could be pulled out, thus permitting the metal gate to rise from its lowered position and allow access to the glass door.

"Finally," Sarah muttered. "And you haven't answered my question."

Chuckling, Valentina bent over, grabbed the handle, and then threw the gate upward. Its metallic rattle echoed in the frigid air.

As she tried to find the other key, which would unlock the glass door, Valentina said, "Atlantic City ain't the most crowded place on Earth this time of year, but that doesn't mean there ain't nobody here, y'know? We might still get clients."

"Who can call us or e-mail us." Sarah was now jumping up and down to keep warm, her hijab sliding back from her forehead a bit. "Which we can answer in your nice warm house in Hammonton."

"We get walk-ins here, especially from people who work the hotels and casinos. They don't like to talk over the phone about this stuff. And their bosses tend to read their e-mails.

There it is!" Valentina found the right key and inserted it into the lock.

Sarah practically ran past Valentina once she got the door open. The office space was small, which was good, as it kept the price down. The rent she paid on this space in Atlantic City would rent an office four times this size in her hometown of Hammonton, which was thirty miles to the west.

But AC also had the clients with the deepest pockets.

Sarah flicked the switch to turn on a fluorescent light in the middle of the ceiling and then moved directly to the space heater that sat atop the minifridge in the corner and put it on high.

Valentina had retrieved the mail from the small metal box next to the front door and then came in and shrugged out of her down coat. "Y'know, it's been, what, five years now since you moved here? You ain't used to Jersey winters yet?"

Warming her hands on the heater as it hummed to life, Sarah glanced back and said, "I come from a desert people, what do you want from me?"

"Last time I checked, it got cold in the desert, too," Valentina said with a chuckle as she went through the mail, tossing all the catalogues and advertisements and political flyers into the garbage can. That left the notice to pay the rent from the landlord and a handwritten envelope.

Holding up the former, she said, "File this, will you please, Sarah?"

Sarah glared at her, obviously not wanting to move away from the heater. She also hadn't taken her coat off yet. Walking over to the desk to snatch the piece of cardboard, she then went to the file cabinet next to the minifridge. "I don't know why they send you these things. You pay the rent electronically."

"I finally *stopped* asking them to not send me those things after the tenth time." Valentina shrugged. "They got a computer system that sends 'em automatically. So I file 'em, just in case there's a problem down the line."

"Have you ever had a problem?"

"Not yet."

"And yet you save every single piece of paper," Sarah said in a long-suffering tone after filing the rent notice with the others in a manila folder and closing the file cabinet drawer.

"You never know when you might need it. Hey, listen to this," Valentina added as she sat down in the leather chair behind her desk. She had opened the handwritten envelope. "It's a thank-you note from the Frank family. Well, it says it's from the Frank family, but it's really from their little girl, Helena. 'Dear Ms. Perrone. Thank you for getting the ghost out of our house. It really made me and Mommy and Daddy happy. We all had a good night's sleep for the first time in forever, and now Mommy and Daddy say I can get a puppy. We love you, Helena Frank.'"

Sarah just stood there, her hands clenched over her heart. "Okay, that is the sweetest thing I've ever heard in my life."

Valentina grinned. "It's the little things."

"So, when do I get to learn how to use weapons?"

With a sigh, Valentina said, "Not this crap again. I told you, I'm more of a magick items kinda gal. Weapons just means people get hurt."

"I was talking with José Maldonado—"

Crossing herself, Valentina said, "*Jesu, Giuseppe, Mari,* do *not* take advice on being a Courser from José. If it was up to him, we'd just shoot everything with that stupid .45 of his. And most of the time, that don't work."

"He also said you always use magick items because your cousin owns the store over on Baltic and Indiana."

"Yeah, I love my cousin Bobby, but you may've noticed I don't actually buy nothin' at his store. I go to Saladin's back home in Hammonton. If nothin' else, Bobby's prices are through the roof 'cause he's gotta pay AC rent. Plus, most of his stuff's garbage, 'cause he sells to tourists."

"I seem to recall a supply of silver sticks you purchased from him last week."

"'Cause Saladin was out, and I needed 'em for those rabid werewolves."

The glass door opened, and a man wearing a very expensive-looking trench coat over a thousand-dollar suit walked in. He removed his Ray-Bans and put them in the inner pocket of his suit jacket. "'Bout time you opened, Val. Been waitin' all mornin'."

After shooting Sarah an I-told-you-so look, Valentina stood up. "We been here, like, fifteen minutes, Rocco, what took you so long to walk in?"

"I been waitin' back at the hotel. I had Freddie across the street keepin' an eye out. He called me when you showed up, and then I drove over."

Sitting back down in her chair, Valentina shook her head. She hadn't noticed anybody across the street, but Freddie could've been in one of the fast-food joints. "Always a pleasure, Rocco. What can I do for you?"

Rocco, however, was staring at Sarah. "Who's this?"

"Oh, sorry. Rocco Amalfitano, head of security for Atlantic Resorts Casino and Hotel, this is my apprentice, Sarah el-Guindi."

Rocco turned to stare confusedly at Valentina. "You got an apprentice? That's, like, a thing?"

"How do you think we get new Coursers?"

"The hell do I know? Maybe you grow 'em in a lab."

Valentina chuckled and indicated the guest chair that faced her desk. "Have a seat, Rocco, and tell me what you need."

As he sat down, Rocco pulled a smartphone out of his trench coat pocket. "We got a thing on the beach. Clients're freakin' out. I need you to get it the hell *off* the beach before the bosses find out."

Sarah asked, "How does anybody even know it's there?"

"Whaddaya mean?" Rocco asked.

"Who would be going on the beach in this weather?"

Rolling his eyes, Rocco said, "Somebody's *always* on the beach. We could have ten feet of snow, and somebody'd be on the beach." He had been fondling the screen of his phone. Finally seeming to find what he needed, he handed the phone to Valentina.

Taking the phone, she stared at the image. A sandy beach dotted with shells in the foreground, breaking waves of blue-green water in the background, and right where the two met, a dark-green-scaled creature that either had two arms and two legs, or four legs—it was hard to tell at that angle—with a large round head, tiny recessed eyes, and a snout that looked vaguely fishlike.

"That's the only picture we got, but at least three clients've seen it. They're sayin' it's the Jersey Devil, if you can believe that garbage."

Valentina handed the phone to Sarah so she could get a look at it. "Aw, c'mon, Rocco, you don't think the Jersey Devil's real?"

"Maybe it is, and maybe it ain't, but I ain't never seen it. And I *seen* some stuff. Why you think I keep comin' back here?"

Shrugging, Valentina said, "My charm and good looks?"

Rocco snorted. "Well, you are pretty good lookin', for a crazy Courser lady."

Sarah handed the phone back to Rocco. "Can you e-mail us the picture, please, Mr. Amalfitano?"

"Absolutely. And hey, call me Rocco. Mr. Amalfitano is what people call me when *they* got a problem, and it gets me all nervous. But *I'm* the one with the problem, so call me Rocco." Rocco started fondling the phone screen again, and then asked Valentina, "Same e-mail address as last time?"

Valentina nodded.

Tapping the phone screen with a flourish, Rocco said, "Sent," and put the phone in his coat pocket. "You know what that thing is?"

"I got a few ideas," Valentina said. "But don't worry, I'll have it off the beach and outta your hair within twenty-four hours."

"Okay, great. So, I don't gotta pay the usual rate for this, right? I mean, it's the off-season."

With a sigh, Valentina then engaged in her least favorite aspect of this job: haggling. It took about a minute and a half for her to convince Rocco that Coursers didn't have an off-season even if casinos did, and for him to agree to her usual payment rate. Or, more accurately, her usual rate for the casinos, which was about twenty percent higher than it was for anyone else, as the casinos could damn well afford it. It was Valentina's way of making up for how the casinos themselves overcharged for so much.

After that, Rocco took his leave. As soon as the door closed, Valentina crossed herself again. "*Jesu, Giuseppe, Mari*, every damn time."

"He always tries to talk down the price?" Sarah asked.

"Yeah. If I charged twice as much, it wouldn't be a helluva lot more than a damn rounding error in the casino's budget, but no, he's gotta try to nickel-and-dime me. And he pulls it every *single* time he hires me." Valentina blew out a breath. "C'mon, we gotta take a trip up to the Pine Barrens."

That brought Sarah up short. "Excuse me? Aren't we going to the beach? Maybe get some tracks, try to figure out what it is?"

"Oh, I already know what it is—it's a mugwump."

Sarah frowned. "Then why didn't you tell Mr. Amalfitano that?"

Chuckling as she got up from her chair, Valentina said, "He said to call him Rocco, remember?"

"I prefer to be formal with our clients," Sarah said primly. "Besides, I hear that name and I expect him to be accompanied by a talking moose named Bullwinkle."

"That's Rocky, not Rocco. Gimme a sec." Valentina went back to use the bathroom.

When she was done, she came out and said, "You should use it, too. We got us an hour drive."

"I'm fine, and you didn't answer my question."

They moved toward the door, Valentina grabbing her coat and switching the light off. "Because this ain't just any mugwump, I'm pretty sure it's a mugwump that I know, and he *really* shouldn't be out like that."

"So why are we going to the Pine Barrens?"

Valentina smiled. "You'll see when we get there."

After locking up the storefront, they went to where Valentina had parked her red Equinox. There was still an hour and forty minutes left on the meter, but there was no sense in wasting time. She beeped the vehicle unlocked and then climbed up into the SUV. As usual, she had to readjust the rear-view mirror — somehow, it always crept back up to a higher angle, when she needed it lower so her five-foot-'one frame could actually see into it.

Navigating the Equinox through downtown until she got to the AC Expressway, she zipped westward down that highway, the vehicle's sound system playing a satellite radio channel dedicated entirely to the works of Bruce Springsteen.

After they went past the interchange with Route 40, Valentina turned down the music a bit. "I ever tell you the history of what we been called?"

"We haven't always been called Coursers?"

"Nope."

"Please, don't tell me that we had an even *more* obscure name?"

Laughing, Valentina said, "No, we used to be called Slayers. Matter of fact, we were called that for centuries, but then a TV show called *Buffy the Vampire Slayer* happened in the 90s. All of a sudden, 'slayer' meant a short blonde chick, and nobody took us seriously. So we changed it to Hunters, but then *Supernatural* became a thing. Plus, honestly? Nobody was real happy with either name. We don't just kill monsters, though I'm guessing we probably used to a lot more then."

"Plus, of course, the term 'hunter' conjures images of overweight white men in flannel and denim wearing ballcaps and carrying rifles to shoot innocent deer."

Valentina shuddered. "Yeah."

"What's wrong?" Sarah asked.

"Sorry, just some bad memories." Out of the corner of her eye, Valentina could see that Sarah was looking at her with a querying expression, which made it clear that her apprentice wasn't going to leave it at that, nor would take "none of your business" for an answer. "I got family out in western Pennsylvania on my Mom's side. We used to go visit, me and my brothers."

"You have brothers?"

"Yeah, Niccolo, who's older, and Antonio's younger. Anyway, Uncle Rodney—he was Aunt Annie's husband—used to *love* to go hunting, and one time we were dumb enough to take our trip right when hunting season started. So, Rodney dragged our asses out at the crack of dawn one Saturday morning. Nicky and Tony loved it; I hated every damn second of it." She smirked. "That's probably why I hate weapons so much."

"Why 'Coursers,' then?"

"It's kind of a hunting term? From the Middle Ages, I think. I don't know, but it's a unique name, at least."

"Because no one knows what it is."

Grinning, Valentina said, "It's us!"

Sarah just stared at her, which Valentina studiously ignored as she merged onto the northbound Garden State Parkway.

After several seconds, Sarah folded her arms, let out a dramatic sigh, and said, "I still say it's a stupid name."

"Yeah, I know you say it's a stupid name. Wanna know how I know you say it's a stupid name? *You keep saying it.* I get it, but it's the name we got, and there's, like, thousands of us who still use it."

"Fine."

Valentina only didn't roll her eyes because she was operating a motor vehicle.

She turned Springsteen back up as she drove north, eventually getting off at Exit 58 for Route 539 north.

Within an hour of departing Atlantic City, they were bouncing down a glorified dirt road. Sarah was gripping the so-called "Jesus bar" above the passenger-side door for dear life.

Sarah's voice was shaky as she cried out, "I thought this was supposed to be an off-road vehicle!"

Valentina focused on the path ahead, grateful that it was still daylight, even more grateful that it hadn't snowed recently. "It is. This is *way* off-road."

"I suggest you add the cost of the new suspension you'll need to the expenses portion of the invoice you send to Mr. Amalfitano!"

"You don't gotta shout," Valentina muttered, though the sound system was also playing "Badlands" very loudly as they careened down the dirt path.

Finally, after driving around a large boulder, she saw their destination. "Here we go."

She brought the Equinox to a halt just in front of a large wooden structure, pulling alongside a very old Ford LTD station wagon with a bumper sticker that read MY OTHER RIDE IS A ZAMBONI.

Sarah was now staring out the windshield, still gripping the Jesus bar despite the vehicle having come to a stop. "You've brought me to a log cabin."

"Yup."

"Though I suppose that's not really a cabin, is it?"

Valentina grinned at her apprentice's look of abject confusion. "No?"

"The word 'cabin' implies something—something small. That place is huge. Though I will grant that it's made out of logs."

Valentina shut the ignition off and got out of the SUV. Sarah did likewise a moment later, continuing to stare at the three-story wooden structure. Well, truly, it was four stories, but the attic level was tiny under the slanted roof—though Valentina knew that Nguyet liked it up there where it was quiet and warm and dark.

There was also a wraparound porch on the third story. On a less frigid day, one of the cabin's occupants would no doubt have been lounging out there. Today, though, the fireplace in the downstairs living room was probably going full bore.

Sarah was still staring as Valentina walked up to the front door and grasped the ornate, dragon-head-shaped wrought-iron door knocker in the center. She knocked three times—the thumping of the dragon's chin against the iron plate nailed to the door echoing through the Barrens.

Valentina looked down and smiled at the familiar welcome mat in front of the door: it was inscribed with the words JUST SO YOU KNOW, IT'S BASICALLY A ZOO IN HERE. Around the words were impressions of paws, hooves, chicken feet, and the like.

A few moments later, the door opened to reveal a tall, winged figure. The wings in question were leathern and lowered as far behind her back as possible. Two horns protruded from the top of her head, pointing up and back, while her long face ended in a snout that pointed down and forward, her mouth filled with sharp teeth.

She had opened the door with a five-fingered hand, each finger ending in a long, pointed talon. The creature's skin was of a similar leathery quality to that of the wings, with tapered bits around the sides of her head, at her elbows, and at one or two other places on her person. A long, thick tail curled behind her, resting on the floor, and her legs bent back at the knee, with the hocks coming straight down to the floor ending in taloned toes.

What amused Valentina the most was the polka-dot apron the creature wore with the words KISS THE COOK emblazoned on the front.

In a deep, hissing voice that sounded like a truck driving over a glass bottle, the creature said, "Ms. Perrone. What brings you here? And who is this?"

Valentina looked over at her apprentice, who stood with mouth agape. "Is—is that—?"

"Quinque Tredecim, this is my apprentice, Sarah el-Guindi. Sarah, this is Quinque, better known to most folks as the Jersey Devil."

Quinque hissed. "Not a popular appellation in *this* house, Ms. Perrone, you know that."

Sarah whirled on Valentina. "You said the Jersey Devil isn't real!"

"When'd I say that?"

"This morning! To Mr. Amalfitano!"

"I didn't, either! What I said was, 'C'mon, Rocco, you don't think the Jersey Devil's real?'"

Folding her arms, Sarah said, "Your phrasing implied that there was no such thing as the Jersey Devil."

"That's what I wanted Rocco to think. Better he only knows about what he's come across, not what he ain't come across. There's enough crazy out there."

Putting her taloned hands on her leathery, apron-covered hips, Quinque asked, "Is there any need for me to be a part of this conversation?"

"Actually, we'd like to come in, if we can, Quinque. It's about Etienne."

"Who's Etienne?" Sarah asked.

Quinque gave another hiss. "I suppose you *should* come inside. Wipe your feet, please."

Inside was a large living room-type area with a high, two-story ceiling, but also a balcony, a wooden staircase to the right leading up to it. Past the staircase was the dining room, and beyond that was the kitchen.

Opposite the front door on the far side of the living room was a fireplace, which was indeed going at full bore. Since the last time Valentina had been here, they'd upgraded from a 45" television to an 85", which hung on the wall right over the fireplace, and currently showing a sports network giving highlights of the previous night's hockey games. Valentina was hoping there'd be news of the Jersey Devils, just for the irony, but instead, they were discussing the previous night's game between the Philadelphia Flyers and the Carolina Hurricanes.

There was a large couch between the door and the fireplace/TV, facing the latter, and Valentina saw a large, white-furred creature on one end of it, an even larger, orange-furred creature on the other side, with a more average-sized green-scaled being in the middle. Perpendicular to the couch was a stool on which sat a skinny, white-skinned figure with large insect wings protruding from his back. A giant spider hung from a web attached to the underside of the balcony, and what looked like a mallosaur was walking across the balcony, entering one of the upper rooms.

Sarah barely made it through the doorway before she stopped short. "What—what *is* this place?"

"My home," Quinque said.

The figure on the stool flew over to the front door. In a whispery voice, he asked, "May I take your coats?"

"Thanks, Jimmy." Valentina shrugged out of her down coat and handed it to the flying man. "How's Maria doing?"

"She's still in Hawai'i. She won't come back until spring at the earliest."

Grinning, Valentina said, "Still allergic to winter, huh?"

"So it would seem," Jimmy said in a long-suffering tone.

Sarah handed Jimmy her coat also. "Thank you," she muttered.

Jimmy flew off to hang them up.

Quinque started moving toward the staircase. "Come with me to the kitchen, please. You may assist me in getting lunch ready."

"Be happy to," Valentina said as they followed Quinque past the staircase.

Sarah turned to Valentina as they walked. "You *know* all these monsters?"

"They ain't monsters, Sarah, they're people."

"That's a sasquatch, a chupacabra, a yeti, and a giant spider watching hockey highlights with an albino with moth wings, plus I don't know *what* that was on the balcony."

They went through the dining room and into the long, wide kitchen area. Both walls were lined with cabinets, and there was a ton of counter space, in addition to two ovens, a five-burner electric stove (one burner of which bore a large pot with a cover slightly askew), two microwaves, a dishwasher, and a huge sink. Valentina smelled the distinctive aroma of chicken and spices that meant Quinque was making chicken stock.

"The guy on the balcony was Izzie," she said to Sarah. "He's a mokele-mbembe."

Quinque took the lid off the soup and grabbed a wooden spoon off the counter to stir it. "He prefers to be called Isembi ever since that argument with Eleutheria."

Valentina rolled her eyes. "Is Ellie back on that 'nicknames are fascist' kick?"

Another hiss from Quinque as she replaced the lid, again leaving it slightly askew. "Which is why she prefers not to be called 'Ellie,' yes."

Not wanting to get into that argument again, especially with Ellie not even in the room, Valentina instead sniffed the air, permeated as it was with the delightful odors of the chicken stock. She recognized a particular spice and asked, "Did you finally remember to put savory in the soup?"

"Yes. You were right, Ms. Perrone, it makes the soup much better."

"I only been tellin' you that a thousand times."

"Indeed." Quinque turned to look at Sarah. "The other four in the living room watching that execrable sports channel are Walter, Armando, Nukilik, and Nguyet. Upstairs, along with Isembi, are Eleutheria, Munish, and Billy-Bob."

Valentina frowned, not recognizing one of the names. Walter was the sasquatch, Armando the chupacabra, Nukilik the yeti, and Nguyet the big spider, while Billy-Bob was a howler and Eleutheria was a bunyip. "Who's Munish?"

"An intelligent primate who was stuck in a zoo in New Delhi. A Courser there was able to arrange to have him brought here."

"Was it Abhaya Batra?"

Quinque shook her head. "No, it was a male Courser."

Abhaya was the only Courser Valentina knew from India. "Well, I'm glad Munish found a home here."

Sarah was standing with her arms folded again. "So this is a sanctuary?"

"Yes," Quinque said. "You used the word 'monster' earlier, Ms. el-Guindi, but that term is not applicable to anyone who lives in my house. No one here has ever willingly harmed another soul, except in extreme self-defense."

"Or what they claim is self-defense," Sarah muttered.

"Excuse me?" This time Quinque's hiss was quite loud.

"You gotta forgive my apprentice," Valentina said quickly.

"I do not believe I *have* to do so at all, Ms. Perrone."

"Her family was killed by an Al-Mi'raj—who claimed he did it in self-defense. She's an apprentice Courser, she's still learning. But she got reason to be suspicious and cynical, y'know?"

Sounding much more contrite, Sarah added, "Having said that, I understand how easy it is to judge someone by appearances. I was four years old when the Twin Towers were destroyed in 2001, and I grew up in the time after that seeing people judge me solely because of this." She pointed at her head, or more specifically at the hijab that covered all but her face. "I apologize, Ms. Tredecim, for the use of the word 'monster' to describe your charges."

Quinque opened her arms in a conciliatory gesture. "Apology accepted, Ms. el-Guindi."

Sarah bowed her head.

Turning to Valentina, Quinque said, "The stock is almost ready. I must start the pasta. Please tell me what you can of Etienne."

As Valentina replied, Quinque went to one of the cabinets and removed a smaller pot, which she then filled with water.

"One of the hotels in Atlantic City hired us to get rid of something that some tourists saw on the beach." She took her smartphone out of her jeans pocket. "They got a pic, and it sure *looks* like Etienne." Calling up the picture in question, she held the phone display-out toward Quinque.

Quinque placed the water-filled pot on the stove and turned the burner on. "That is, indeed, Etienne. He has been missing for a day, but he sometimes goes for long walks in the Barrens. I discourage the practice, but there are times when we suffer from cabin fever and must leave the confines of these wooden walls." Quinque let out a very long hiss. "However, Etienne knows he is not to leave the Pine Barrens. Please, Ms. Perrone, I would be grateful if you returned him home."

"That was always gonna be the plan once I made sure it was really him."

"Thank you. Would you like to stay for lunch?" Quinque went to another cabinet to remove a bag of imported Italian rigatoni as she asked the question.

It almost physically hurt Valentina to say, "I'm sorry, we can't," given that she'd been smelling how heavenly the soup was since they came into the kitchen, and that she was the one who'd recommended the imported pasta to Quinque. "Getting here and back has already eaten two hours into the time we need to get Etienne off the beach, and the client wants us to move our butts. Can you save me a little? I'll take it when we bring Etienne back."

"Very well." Quinque looked at Sarah. "Enough for two?"

Sarah shook her head. "I do not consume meat. But thank you for the offer."

Quinque nodded in understanding and then led them back into the living room.

The TV now showed highlights of a game between the Montréal Canadiens and the Detroit Red Wings.

"James, will you please get our guests' coats?" Quinque asked.

Nodding, Jimmy flew toward the back of the cabin.

The yeti turned to face them. "Leaving so quickly, Val? We were gonna watch a movie over lunch."

"Sorry, Nuke, but we gotta go fetch Etienne."

Rolling his eyes, the sasquatch asked, "What'd that stupid mugwump do this time?"

"Go out in public," Valentina said. "But we'll bring him home, Walter, don't you worry."

"I ain't worried." Walter snorted, which sounded like a pipe bomb exploding. "It's his own stupid fault. He's gonna get his ass shot, he's not careful."

"Or worse," Armando said, "become dinner."

Nguyet made what sounded like a spitting noise from his web and said, "No human would eat him, he's too gamey."

"Thought you liked gamey meat," Walter said.

"Which is why I said no *human* would eat him. Not," he added quickly, perhaps noticing the murderous look on Quinque's leathery face, "that I would ever even entertain the possibility of consuming poor Etienne. He is, after all, our housemate."

"As I have said before," Quinque said in a hard voice, "I do not wish such subjects discussed, not even in a jocular manner."

"Yes, ma'am," Walter said.

"Here you go," Jimmy said, flying back with both coats and holding them out for the Coursers.

"Thanks, Jimmy," Valentina said, taking her down coat and sliding into it. "Hopefully, we'll get Etienne back in time for dinner."

"That is also *my* hope," Quinque said quietly.

After saying their goodbyes to the assembled multitudes, the Coursers went back out to the Equinox.

Glancing at the station wagon, Sarah asked, "Which ones drive?"

Valentina grinned. "Just Armando."

"That's the chupacabra?"

Nodding, Valentina beeped the car unlocked and climbed into the Equinox. Once again readjusting the mirror, she started the ignition, and backed up a bit, so she was past the station wagon, then turned around and headed back down the dirt road.

"If we're in such a hurry," Sarah said, "why did we take the time to drive all this way? We could have simply called."

"You can only call somebody that's got a phone."

Sarah's eyes widened. "No phones?"

Valentina shook her head. "They're completely off the grid. Electricity in the cabin comes from a generator they got out back. And Armando may know how to drive, but he ain't got a license, neither."

Once again clutching the Jesus bar for dear life as they bounced away from the cabin, Sarah asked, "You have obviously known of this place for some time since you are friendly with the occupants and have given Ms. Tredecim cooking advice. Not—" She actually smiled at this point. "—that that's an indicator, since you give cooking advice to total strangers, given half the chance."

"Food is important," Valentina muttered defensively.

"You seemed to think that that Indian Courser you mentioned knew of this sanctuary. Is it known to all Coursers?"

"No," Valentina said emphatically as she swerved the Equinox around a divot. "A bunch of us here in Jersey know about it, and a few others 'round the world, but a bunch don't, and the Wardein don't, either."

"Really?" Sarah sounded surprised at that, and Valentina couldn't blame her. All magickal activity in a particular geographic region was managed by a Wardein. Indeed, Wardeins hired Coursers more than any one client, for the most part.

"Yeah, really. David's a good guy, don't get me wrong, but he's old-school, and he's the type who sees that cabin and figures we should toss a magickal nuke at it." Central and southern New Jersey was the demesne of David Averbach, who'd been Wardein of the region for almost five decades. "And another thing—you breathe one syllable about Quinque to José, and you and I are done for good. Got it?"

"I was, in fact, just going to ask if José was among those in the inner circle."

"Absolutely no damn way. He'd be who David would hire to nuke the place."

"How long have this select group of Coursers known about it?"

"More than a hundred years, now." Valentina turned the Equinox down another dirt path, which would lead to an actual road, which would lead to Route 70. "How much do you know about the Jersey Devil?"

"Only that the myth is pervasive enough to lead the local hockey team to name themselves for it. Or, rather, her."

"This one's a her, they aren't all."

Sarah's eyes grew wide. "There are more than one?"

"Yup." Valentina came to a stop when the path intersected with a narrow, but blessedly paved road, waited for a pickup truck to go past, then turned left onto the road.

Sarah let go of the Jesus bar. "Where are the others?"

"Oh, there ain't any others right now. May as well tell you the whole story."

"From a hundred years ago? When we were called Slayers?"

"Yup. Specifically, in early 1909."

Chapter Two

The rising sun blazed through Josiah Clevenger's bedroom window, its light immediately waking him, as it did every morning. No matter when he took to bed the night before, dawn's early light always served to rouse him from his slumber. This morning's sun was brighter than usual, with the light reflecting off the snow that remained on the ground since the storm of a week earlier.

His dreams had been turbulent, as usual, but upon awakening, he could no longer recall the details, also as usual. The life of a Slayer was full of wonders and horrors, so that was not much of a surprise. His sister Emmelina had been reading the works of alienists, and she said that his dreams were his mind attempting to make sense of the madness he encountered in his travails.

For his part, Josiah would rather Emmelina had gone back to reading novels. They were trash, but at least they didn't prompt lectures on his health and well-being.

He climbed out from under the quilt that Mother had made for him all those years ago. Another hole had developed in one of the seams, and Josiah reminded himself to ask Emmelina to repair it, a reminder that he knew he would not recall by the time he saw her next.

The cold of a New Jersey winter wracked Josiah's bones, and he moved quickly to change from his nightgown into his day clothes. He had no Slayer business today, at least not yet.

That could change, of course. In certain circles, it was known that one of the owners of Clevenger's Dry Goods was a Slayer, and sometimes patronage came from those ostensibly there to shop. And tomorrow night was to be a new moon, and that sometimes meant such work.

After buttoning his flannel shirt and lacing his boots, he clasped the Horvath amulet around his neck. A gift from the Slayer who trained him, the amulet detected the active presence of magick, and he only took it off when he slept, and then only because he feared being strangled by the chain.

He put the pouch with the cash for the till into his pack. Tossing the sack over his shoulder, he left the room he rented to go down to the ground floor of the boarding house, where the landlady, Mrs. Van Leuwen, was preparing breakfast.

"Good morning, Mr. Clevenger," Mrs. Van Leuwen said from the kitchen as he clomped down the stairs, his boots echoing in the stairwell. She didn't even look up to verify that it was him. There was no need — none of the other boarders were ever up this early, except perhaps Mr. Pratt, and then only if the author had been awake through the night.

Sure enough, as Josiah turned the corner to enter the kitchen, he saw that Mr. Elois Pratt was seated at the table, sipping coffee and reading over a sheet of paper. More sheets of paper were piled next to him.

"Morning, Clevenger," Pratt said, briefly glancing up from his reading.

"How goes the novel, Pratt?" Josiah asked.

"I thought I had finally determined the nature of the climax and was up through much of the night getting it down. But now I sit here in the cold light of day, and I fear that the night's muse has given way to the morning's disappointment."

Josiah took a seat across from the author. "Then you have *not* determined the nature of the climax?"

"Apparently not." He swallowed the rest of his coffee. "Mrs. Van Leuwen, a refill, if you please?"

Mrs. Van Leuwen made a *tch* noise. "The new pot is almost finished, Mr. Pratt, and you drank all of the previous one. Perhaps you should abstain and get some sleep."

"Not until I have read all of my night's labors, Mrs. Van Leuwen, and determined where I went so horribly wrong."

Shaking her head and making yet another *tch* noise, the steel-gray-haired landlady grabbed a spatula and used it to shovel the eggs she'd been cooking out of the frying pan and onto a plate, which she brought to Josiah. "The coffee will be ready shortly, Mr. Clevenger."

"So I heard you inform our resident scribe. My thanks, ma'am."

Bowing her head, Mrs. Van Leuwen retreated to the stove, wiping her hands on the apron that protected her house dress from the vagaries of food preparation. She began her preparations for the later breakfasts that would be required for the boarders.

"Have you heard the latest, Clevenger?" Pratt asked. "They're saying the Leeds Devil is back. I saw the newspaper article over the weekend. Strange footprints in the snow."

"According to today's paper," Mrs. Van Leuwen said, "the demon's been seen killing chickens. They called it a Wozzle Bug."

Swallowing his eggs, Josiah said, "I have found that the newspapers are half misnamed. They are, in fact, made of paper, but rarely do they deliver actual news. There is, I can assure you, no such thing as a Wozzle Bug or a Leeds Devil or whatever it is the papers claim."

"But there were witnesses, Mr. Clevenger!" Mrs. Van Leuwen said with fervor. "Good Christian men described the Wozzle Bug. It walked on its hind legs, it has wings, and has the body of a kangaroo."

"I read," Pratt added, "that it has the head of a horse and can breathe fire from its nostrils."

"Balderdash, all of it."

In truth, Josiah couldn't speak with authority that this *wasn't* some supernatural creature. However, he had read the same newspaper account that Mrs. Van Leuwen had, and the prints in the snow described therein bore no resemblance to any monster of which Josiah was aware.

Having said that, there were plenty of monsters of which he was unaware—his career as a Slayer had introduced him to many a creature new to his ken—but still, he had his doubts about the so-called "Leeds Devil."

Especially given the source.

Still, he maintained the public fiction that he was only a simple shopkeeper, at least to those unaware of the eldritch world that existed out of sight of most. It behooved him to maintain that fiction by expressing public skepticism for these claims about the so-called Wozzle Bug. Especially to Mrs. Van Leuwen, who might see his vocation as a Slayer as a reason to forbid him from continuing to lodge in her boarding house.

After finishing his breakfast, including Mrs. Van Leuwen's strong coffee, he grabbed his pack, retrieved his hat, coat, and scarf from the closet by the front door, and braved the winter morning.

Bitterly cold air blew in off the Delaware River, slicing through the wool of Josiah's coat. Behind his neck, his scarf flapped in the breeze parallel to the ground. The heels of his boots crunched in the snow that had yet to melt. He wondered if more snow was coming.

Turning the corner, he saw the sprawling complex of the New York Shipbuilding Company. When Josiah's parents opened their store in 1852, the front of the shop had overlooked the river, but when New York Shipbuilding broke ground in 1899, the building raised blocked the sight. While Josiah missed his parents every day, he also was grateful that, at the very least, they didn't live long enough to see their lovely view spoiled.

Well, in truth, only Father would have complained about that. Mother would have welcomed the increased clientele for the store. In fact, business had improved tremendously with the arrival, not just of New York Ship, but also the Campbell Soup Company and many other manufacturers. Indeed, Camden had been at the vanguard of what the intelligentsia on the lecture circuit had referred to as the "industrial revolution," which had increased the population a hundredfold.

Which meant not just more people purchasing dry goods at the store, but also more business for Josiah as a Slayer.

A small price to pay for a spoiled view. At least, that was what he had told himself lo, these ten years.

One change necessitated by the increased populace of the municipality was the need to place a padlock on the front door to the store when the business was not open. Emmelina had insisted upon it, but Josiah had resisted, right up until the moment when someone entered the store in the night and stole three bags of horse feed.

The Clevengers hadn't reported that particular transgression to the constabulary. The police were, truly, of little use in such matters, and both Josiah and Emmelina had assumed that the thieves were in desperate need of something to feed their horses — or themselves.

Still, they could hardly allow the store to be burgled on any kind of regular basis, and so Josiah gave in to Emmelina's entreaties and purchased a padlock.

He unlocked it with a snap, and then went in through the door. After hanging his coat, hat, and scarf on the coat rack by the front door, he then proceeded to get the store ready for customers.

One reason why they had avoided expanding their merchandise to include more perishable items was ease of storage. It also meant that to open the store, he merely had to check to make sure all the signs denoting price and item description were in place and accurate. As it happened, the sign for the coffee beans had fallen to the floor, and Josiah needed to replace it.

He then went through the usual routine with the cash register, a newfangled piece of equipment Josiah had again resisted purchasing, but Emmelina had insisted. First, he pushed the button labeled NO SALE. Then he pulled the lever that was supposed to open the cash drawer. The drawer then opened only half an inch and stopped. Josiah then smacked the left-hand side of the register. The drawer then opened all the way. He made a mental note to complain to Emmelina about it when she came down at midday.

Said mental note was, as ever, a waste of effort, as Josiah would no more recall to make that complaint than he would to tell his sister about the hole in the quilt.

He removed the greenbacks from the pouch in his pack and divided them by denomination in the till, then did the same for the coins. In addition, he placed the padlock in the back of the drawer for safekeeping until Emmelina closed the store that night.

The morning passed by quietly, with many of their regular customers coming in. Mr. Dermott to purchase a bag of coffee beans for use in one of the manufacturing plant's canteen. Mrs. Wilberforce to obtain bolts of fabric with which to sew dresses for her daughters. Miss Abruzzi to buy flour for her mother. And Mr. Kawalski to pick up some more saddle soap for his horses' tack.

As usual, there was neighborhood gossip, though Josiah was surprised it all consisted of the same subject brought up by Pratt at the breakfast table.

"Did y'hear about the devil roamin' the streets?" Mr. Dermott asked. "Comes straight from the gates of hell, and that's the truth."

"My daughters are staying home from the schoolhouse today," Mrs. Wilberforce declared. "I'll not have them taken by some manner of wild beast."

"Is a very strange t'ing," Miss Abruzzi said in her heavily accented voice. She was still learning English. "I hear they put, ah, *cani*?" She shook her head. "Dogs, *si*, dogs on the *diavolo di* Leeds, but they no find."

"Heard they saw that Jabberwock in Pennsauken," Mr. Kawalski said. "Sent a posse after 'em. Didn't think they still had posses, but there it is."

When the sun was at its zenith, Emmelina entered the store from the back room through the swinging doors, which flapped open with a creak as she came in. She kept a small apartment in the back and worked the afternoon alongside Josiah and the evenings alone. Because Josiah's Slayer work often kept him out at night, it made more sense for his time at the store to be the earlier shift.

That was why, when the fire burned down the house they grew up in, claiming the lives of their parents and of Emmelina's husband, Josiah had let Emmelina have the small living quarters adjacent to the store, so she would not have to walk alone at night to a home off-site.

Josiah knew better than most how dangerous the night could be.

The apartment was only two rooms, far too small for two people to live in unless they shared a marriage bed. So, Josiah left it to Emmelina while he rented his room at Mrs. Van Leuwen's.

Emmelina was holding the day's newspaper, which a delivery boy left at her door on the side of the store every morning.

"Good day, Jed. Have you seen the news?"

"And good day to you too, Emmy. I have *heard* the news— according to every customer we've had thus far, the Leeds Devil is roaming the entirety of the region, wreaking havoc on the citizenry."

Tilting her head, Emmelina said, "You don't believe it?"

"I'm—skeptical. I prefer to hear from reliable sources, which neither the customers' gossipmongering nor the newspapers are likely to provide."

"Well, according to today's accounts, the New Jersey Devil—"

"Ha!" Josiah shook his head. "Yet another appellation to add to the list."

"—devoured the dog of Mr. and Mrs. Schmitt of Pennsauken. Mr. Schmitt described the creature as appearing like an opossum, albeit with wings and very sharp teeth."

The conversation was cut short by a young boy entering the store and asking after shirts. Emmelina took him to the long rack in the back of the store where they kept ready-made men's clothes.

Shortly thereafter, a man in what looked to be a well-tailored suit under his topcoat came in. Removing his hat, he placed it on top of the coat rack, as was proper, and then approached the counter, tugging at the ends of his thick mustache as he did so.

"Might you be Mr. Josiah Clevenger?"

Smiling, Josiah said, "I might be, yes, though it would perhaps depend on the reasons why you're asking for me by name."

Sotto voce, the man said, "I have need to retain the services of a Slayer."

"I see. Please, hang up your coat and then come with me."

After the man in the suit removed his coat and hung it up, Josiah could see the suit in its entirety. This was very much a man of wealth who now followed Josiah toward the back of the store. The Slayer exchanged a quick, knowing glance with his sister, who nodded in acknowledgment before turning to assist the boy with his purchase of shirts.

Josiah led the man through the swinging doors into the vestibule. This rectangular space had three other doorways: one leading to the storage room, one leading to Emmelina's apartment, and one leading to the area out back, which contained the privy. Within the space was a couch and a chair, and Josiah indicated the former while he took a seat on the latter. A small end table sat next to the chair with an ashtray atop it and a humidor inside one of the drawers, which Josiah opened.

"You have the better of me, sir," Josiah said as he removed a cigar and a box of matches. "Cigar?"

"No, thank you, I cannot abide the taste of cigars. However, if I may?" He took a gold cigarette case out of his jacket's inner pocket.

Josiah nodded. He bit off one end of the cigar and then pulled a match from the box and struck it against the arm of his chair, lighting it. First, he lit the gentleman's cigarette, then his own cigar. After a morning filled with inane gossip, the soothing taste of the cigar was a welcome palliative.

Puffing the smoke back into the air between them, Josiah said, "Still, sir, you have the better of me."

Bowing his head, the gentleman replaced the cigarette case, then reached into the jacket's other inner pocket and pulled out a smaller case, which contained his calling cards. Retrieving one such card, he handed it over.

Josiah read the black lettering on the white card, which simply read, MARCUS A. GRIMWADE, ESQ., ATTORNEY-AT-LAW.

"I assume," Josiah said as he set the card down on the end table, "that you are here in your capacity as an attorney?"

"Yes." Grimwade took a puff of his cigarette. "I represent Joseph Campbell and Company, and we wish to hire you to track down the creature that the newspapers are calling the New Jersey Devil."

Josiah almost coughed on his cigar. "I beg your pardon?"

"I believe it is sometimes referred to as the Leeds Devil, for some reason."

"There is a belief," Josiah said, "that a Quaker woman from Leeds Point gave birth to the creature."

"I take it, sir, that you do not share that belief?"

Josiah took a puff of his cigar. "I believe that Mr. William Shakespeare said it best, Mr. Grimwade: there are more things in heaven and Earth than are dreamt of in our philosophy. I have seen many things in my time as a Slayer that were most assuredly *not* dreamt of in my philosophy before I took on this calling."

Grimwade regarded Josiah with a raised eyebrow. "That does not answer my question, sir."

Now Josiah grinned. "I suppose it does not. Leave us say that I keep an open mind. However, I must ask you what evidence you have that this devil exists."

Pausing to inhale his cigarette and then tap out the ashes into the ashtray, Grimwade finally said, "I must admit, Mr. Clevenger, I shared your obvious skepticism regarding the creature, dismissing it as the ravings of journalists attempting to sell their sheets to a less-than-discriminating public. However, I was forced to alter my view when I was approached by Mr. Campbell Speelman—the son of one of our company's founders."

Josiah frowned. "One of? I was under the impression that the company was founded by Mr. Joseph Campbell."

"In fact, it was founded by Mr. Campbell and his partner, Mr. Abraham Anderson, in the year of our Lord 1869. While Mr. Anderson divested himself of the partnership seven years later, his son, Mr. Speelman, has continued to work for the company. Mr. Speelman owns an automobile, and so he travels to and from Campbell headquarters here in Camden and his home in Pemberton. Yesterday, when Mr. Speelman arrived at work, he spoke with disdain—I would say, the very same disdain with which you spoke of the Leeds Devil moments ago, Mr. Clevenger—of other residents of Pemberton. Specifically, he spoke of mill workers, who refused to traverse the Pine Barrens for fear of being attacked by the creature."

Tapping ashes from his cigar into the ashtray, Josiah said, "I assume by his commissioning you to hire me that something changed his mind?"

Grimwade nodded. "When he arrived home from work last night, he saw the creature in question. It was breaking into his henhouse."

"What happened?"

"He chased the creature away with his rifle."

Josiah raised an eyebrow. "He shot it?"

Wincing, Grimwade said, "More accurate to say he shot *at* it. He said it will take weeks to extract the buckshot from the henhouse wall, and not a bit of it struck the creature in question."

"I see."

"Mr. Speelman feels that this monster, whatever it may be called, is a danger to the good people of the Delaware Valley and wishes it to be dealt with. That is where you come in."

Josiah took a final puff of his cigar and then placed it in the ashtray. "I don't suppose Mr. Speelman has a description?"

"He has something better: a sketch of the creature. Mr. Speelman is the creative director of the company—indeed, he designed their soup cans."

"And this sketch is where?"

Grimwade smirked slightly. "We will have it couriered to you, should you actually take the job. Mr. Speelman was—reluctant to employ your services, as his belief in such things has never been strong prior to last night."

"Yours is?" Josiah asked with a smirk of his own.

"Oh, yes." Grimwade shuddered as he inhaled the last of his cigarette, then put it out in the ashtray. "You probably don't remember, Mr. Clevenger, but you saved my mother's life from a nixie some five years ago."

"Yes, of course," Josiah said, though he didn't remember the specific case. He'd dealt with several nixies over the years.

"I recommended you on the strength of your work then, but Mr. Speelman wished me to ascertain your willingness to take the commission before releasing the sketch to you. He would prefer not to add to the rumors and tall tales and so wishes to be sure you are unimpeachable."

Josiah nodded. "You can be assured of my discretion, Mr. Grimwade, as you may be equally assured that I will deal with this creature."

"Excellent." Grimwade again tugged on the ends of his mustache.

After discussing monetary terms, Grimwade took his leave, promising to send a messenger with the sketch by the end of the business day.

As the lawyer left, Josiah saw that Emmelina was wrapping up two shirts in parchment for the boy, who handed over several coins in payment.

Once the boy departed the store, Emmelina regarded Josiah with concern. "I take it that that fancy-dressed gentleman had work for you as a Slayer?"

Josiah nodded. "And it seems this creature that has everyone all a-twitter might be real as well." He shared Grimwade's story of Campbell Speelman's henhouse intruder. "I shall need to hire a horse and then travel to the places where the devil has been sighted."

"Luckily, Jed, you have a very smart sister."

Frowning, Josiah asked, "What do you mean?"

"I suspected that it would not be long before someone hired you to seek out this Jersey Devil, and so I have compiled a list of all the places it has been seen, according to the newspaper accounts."

Josiah let out a hearty laugh. " I can always count on you, Emmy. If you'd be so kind as to provide that list—after you've added Pemberton to it. Meantime, I'm going to go to Mr. Kawalski and see about a horse, and also call upon Miss Silverio."

"And I will send for young Master Oliver to see if he is available to mind the store for the next few mornings."

That brought Josiah up short. "Few? Do you believe this will require more than a day's work?"

"Jed, the list I am to give you includes Philadelphia, Collingswood, Hammonton, Millville, Burlington, and now also Pemberton, not to mention right here in Camden. It will take you several days merely to reach all those locales, query the citizenry, and track the monster down."

"I suppose you are correct."

With a sigh, Josiah put his hat, coat, and scarf on and departed the store. First, he went to Kawalski's Stables and negotiated for the renting of a horse for a few days. Unsurprisingly, Mr. Kawalski preferred to be paid in horse feed. Disappointingly, Sylvan Wye—an Arabian Josiah had enjoyed riding many times in the past—was not available, but Mr. Kawalski promised a good steed would be provided come the morning.

His next stop was Marianina Silverio, who owned a small house on the outskirts of Camden. Most knew her as an apothecary, but she was also the finest supplier of magickal items this side of the Delaware River.

Miss Silverio had inherited the business from her mother, Grazia. Mrs. Silverio had been a licensed seller of magickal items in her native Italy until she, her husband, and her infant daughter emigrated to the United States along with many others twenty years before. Mr. Silverio had died of a fever while traversing the Atlantic. Grazia had raised Marianina alone here in Camden, training her to take over the family business when she died, which she did of consumption only two years earlier.

While Josiah had not wished ill on Grazia, truly, he was grateful that he now only had to deal with her daughter. The Widow Silverio had been frightening, and he had had an irrational fear that she was going to turn him into a forest animal every time he visited. He had no such fear now visiting her daughter.

"*Ciao, Signor* Clevenger," Miss Silverio said upon Josiah's entering the small house. Even as Miss Silverio spoke, she rose from the rocking chair where she had been doing some knitting. Her black cat, Stregata, meowed at him and rubbed up against his boot.

"Good day to you, Miss Silverio," Josiah said as he reached down to rub Stregata's head.

"What may I do for you today, *Signor*?"

"Have you heard the tales of the Leeds Devil?"

Shrugging, Miss Silverio said, "I have read the accounts in the newspapers."

"Well, it would appear to be real."

"Which one?" She let out a musical laugh. "As I say, I have read the accounts in the newspapers, and I have found that no two of them are the same."

"I cannot say for sure, but I have a client who has seen it and is willing to provide a drawing of what he saw. What I need from you is something that will allow me to either bind it or harm it — preferably both."

Miss Silverio let out a slight hissing noise. "I know not what the creature is, so I know not how to bind it. As for harming, I have found that silver is often, ah, *pericoloso* — harmful to *i mostri*."

Josiah had been afraid of this but had to at least try. "In that case, I will require a box of silver .44 caliber rimfire."

"Ah, still using the Henry rifle, *si*?"

"It has served me quite well. More so when armed with your silver ammunition."

"Is it always that you kill what you hunt?"

"We are called Slayers for a reason, Miss Silverio," Josiah said gravely. "What we hunt are creatures of the devil, trying to do harm to good people. It is my function to stop them by any means necessary. Those means often require the use of my Henry rifle."

"Are we not people of reason who may talk and find a solution?"

"This is war," Josiah said. He didn't add, *a war that has gone on for millennia.*

"*Si*, and wars end when men sit at a table and bargain over the terms of peace."

"If scripture teaches us nothing else, Miss Silverio," Josiah said quietly, "it is that attempts to bargain with Satanic forces always end badly."

She smiled, then. "And yet you speak well, *signor*. Most Slayers would find my questions offensive and tell me to—how did that one gentleman put it? Ah, yes, 'be quiet and fetch my magick, woman!'"

"Disagreeing with someone is no excuse for being impolite to a lady, Miss Silverio." He bowed slightly.

She inclined her head with a smile. "*Grazie.* I will now be quiet and fetch your magick." Moving toward the back of the house, she added, "I have something else for you as well."

"Oh?" he said, but she had already disappeared into the back room.

Stregata was still rubbing his boot and meowing, so Josiah knelt to rub the cat's head some more, lamenting the fact that Mrs. Van Leuwen refused to allow animals in her boarding house.

Miss Silverio returned from the back, holding a wooden box and a velvet pouch. "Stregata likes you," she said with amazement.

Josiah stood back up. "Is that so odd?"

"It is, yes. She is *un gatto antipatico*. I do not know the word in English."

"Unpleasant?"

"Possibly." She held out the two items. "These are for you. The box is the silver bullets for your Henry rifle."

Taking both items, Josiah noted that the pouch was not only velvet but weighed almost nothing. "And the other?"

"Do not open the pouch until you are in the presence of a winged creature. When you do open it, its wings will be restrained for one day."

The one consistency throughout all the descriptions of this monster was its wings. "Thank you, Miss Silverio."

"*Prego, Signor* Clevenger. I hope you are successful in your endeavor."

While *en route* to Mr. Kawalski's to pick up his horse the next morning, Josiah read a copy of the *Inquirer*, a newspaper from Philadelphia. The headline on the front page read: WHAT-IS-IT VISITS ALL SOUTH JERSEY. There was even a photograph of hoofprints in the snow in Burlington.

Armed with his Henry rifle, silver bullets, the velvet pouch, and the sketch of the creature, which had been delivered to the store the previous evening, Josiah rode a fine light-brown-coated steed named Sunlight to Pemberton to talk to Mr. Speelman's domestic staff and investigate the henhouse.

The one thing he was able to determine, thanks to the Horvath amulet, was that there was no active presence of magick. All that meant was that this Jersey Devil was not a human who'd been transformed into a monster, nor did it wield magick — or, at least, it hadn't while it menaced Mr. Speelman's livestock.

While most of the domestics corroborated Mr. Speelman's story, the cook had an additional tale to tell.

"That weren't the only time I saw that there monster, I can tell you that."

Intrigued, Josiah asked, "When else did you see it, ma'am?"

"Oh, pish-tosh, I ain't no 'ma'am.' Call me Cook, s'what everyone do. And I saw it again this morn', I did, right at the break of dawn! But it weren't like the first time, when it barreled through like an elephant in a china shop, no sir. This time it were — I dunno, *careful*-like. Seemed to be lookin' for something, I can tell you that."

"You're sure it was the same creature?"

"You think there could be two like that? No, sir, it was the very same demonspawn of Satan that flew in on those bat-wings and with those horrible talons. I'm guessin' it left something behind when Mr. Speelman chased it off, and it came back a-lookin' for it."

Josiah nodded his assent to this theory, but he wasn't entirely convinced. He quietly wondered if the creature was being sought by another of its kind in much the same way Josiah was searching for it.

He was very grateful to have obtained plenty of enchanted ammunition for his Henry rifle. While he had no way of knowing if the silver bullets would affect this Jersey Devil, he had found that such weaponry tended to work more often than not against the creatures he pursued.

He was finished by midday. Mr. Speelman's stable boy had taken good care of Sunlight, feeding and watering him. Josiah tipped the boy a penny, re-mounted, and rode back west.

By late afternoon, he had reached Haddon Heights and noticed that there was a crowd gathered around a trolley car. Men from the county sheriff were present, including a deputy Josiah knew.

Aloysius McInerny's family had had some unfortunate dealing with the fae. Josiah had helped them through that, and Deputy McInerny had been very grateful. So, Josiah knew he could count on a true answer to a query of what was happening from him, an assurance he wouldn't normally have from officials of law and government, who tended to be tragically literal-minded.

Indeed, the first thing McInerny said as Josiah dismounted from Sunlight and walked the horse toward the outskirts of the scene was, "Not surprised to be seein' you here, Clevenger. This looks like your kind of donnybrook."

"Good to see you, McInerny. What happened here?"

"'Tis the Devil of Leeds, as sure as I'm standin' here. It jumped on yonder trolley car and frightened the passengers somethin' horrible. Young Franklin over there," he indicated one of the other deputies, "was nearby and fired his pistol, but to no avail."

"When did this happen?"

"'Twas not half an hour gone."

Josiah cursed to himself. He'd just missed it. "May I speak with the passengers?"

McInerny nodded. "I'll clear the way for you."

The chief deputy had been about to let the passengers go on their way, but McInerny convinced him to let Josiah speak to them. "He's an investigator," McInerny said gravely.

Josiah smiled. It wasn't the first time someone had referred to him thusly, hoping to invoke notions of his being a Pinkerton or some such. He was more than happy to take advantage of that famous private detective agency's reputation to make his own work easier. After tying his horse to a nearby trough about half-filled with water, Josiah went to speak with these witnesses to the latest sighting of the Jersey Devil.

The trolley-car passengers were all quite agog.

"It looked like a giant, flying kangaroo, if you can believe such a thing."

"I didn't get a great look at it, but it definitely had wings. Nasty beast."

"It was a dragon! A real-live dragon! Right there on the roof of the trolley!"

"I swear it was a cross between an alligator and a bat!"

"Please, sir, I must find myself some whiskey, that I may forget everything that occurred here this afternoon. I was a teetotaler until today, and then I saw that—that *thing* land upon the roof, straight from the gates of hell!"

Again, nothing from the Horvath amulet. Which meant this was a simple demon, probably accidentally let loose from whatever nether realm demons came from.

After thanking both McInerny and the chief deputy for their assistance, Josiah untied Sunlight, his chin wet from making use of the trough, and rode out of town.

He'd not had a proper meal since Mrs. Van Leuwen's breakfast, aside from some jerky from his own store's supply that he'd noshed on earlier. Therefore, he decided to stop in Collingswood, specifically at a steak house on Haddon Avenue, a thoroughfare that would take him back into Camden directly after his meal.

Collingswood was also on Emmelina's list of towns where the Jersey Devil had been sighted, so over the course of the meal, he queried the restaurant's staff, as well as several fellow patrons, about whether or not they had seen the monster in question.

Not surprisingly, most everyone had a story.

"Oh, aye, I saw the blessed thing. Looked like some kind of ostrich, it did! Someone summoned the fire brigade, and they turned their hoses on it, but then it flew away, it did! Damndest thing you ever saw!"

"Yeah, I saw it. Flew off toward Moorestown, I think."

"It attacked my aunt's cat!"

"My *mamusia* says she saw it trying to eat our chickens, but she is always saying that things are eating our chickens. It was the neighbor's dog last week."

"Balderdash! Stuff and nonsense! No such thing as the Leeds Devil, and that's a fact! I'm sure that what I saw running down the alleyway behind the cobbler's was merely a kangaroo that escaped from the Philadelphia Zoo."

It was late evening when he finally arrived home. By the light of the electric streetlamps on Haddon, he saw a boy putting up signs on those selfsame lampposts, as well as on some of the walls. Josiah steered Sunlight over to one sign.

It was from the Philadelphia Zoo, offering a $10,000 reward for the capture of the Leeds Devil.

Josiah stared at the sign for several seconds.

That was a considerable sum of money. He and Emmelina had been talking about expanding the store, building a second story atop it that would contain an apartment large enough for both of them to reside in, and then use the space currently occupied by Emmelina's living quarters to expand the size of the selling space.

All that had been stopping them was a lack of funds and an unwillingness to be beholden to the bank for a loan, which they would then demand back with interest.

This reward would enable them to not only make those changes to the store and save Josiah the expense of Mrs. Van Leuwen's boarding house but also enable them to put some money aside. For *that*, Josiah was more than happy to use the bank, as the interest would be in *their* favor.

And it wouldn't even be a conflict with his client. Grimwade's commission was solely that the Devil be dealt with. Turning it over to the Philadelphia Zoo would accomplish that.

"You think they'll capture the thing?"

Josiah turned to see the boy who'd been putting up the signs. "I don't know," he said, "but this is certainly a motivator."

"Not for me, it ain't," the boy said with a shudder. "I heard tell a group'a ten men went after it in Pennsauken, and they weren't never heard from again!"

"Really?" Josiah recalled Mr. Kawalski saying something similar.

"Aye, 'twere in the paper, it was!" The boy pulled a rolled-up newspaper out of his back pocket and unrolled it. The paper was open to the story, which told of ten farmers who tracked the Jabberwock before disappearing.

This was the first time someone had gone missing. It might have been nothing, but it looked like he'd be taking Sunlight to Pennsauken in the morning.

"That's pretty dire," he said to the boy for lack of anything better to say. "You'd best finish your business and get on home."

"Aye. Good evenin' to you, mister!" The boy gave a sloppy salute and then ran down Haddon Avenue to continue his work.

Just as he was about to kick Sunlight into a trot to get him home, Josiah heard what sounded like a woman crying out: "Help! Police! Help! Help! My poor baby!"

He quickly rode Sunlight toward the cry, which came from a small house belonging to Mrs. Mary Sorbiski. She came into the store sometimes, and he knew she lived alone, though she was referred to by one and all by the honorific of "Mrs." Whether her lonely state was due to widowhood or some other reason, he knew not.

She stood in front of her house, clutching her dog to her breast with her right hand while holding a broom in her left. Josiah couldn't identify the canine's breed, but the animal was obviously traumatized, whimpering into Mary's sweater, which she wore over her nightclothes. As he rode closer, he saw that the dog was bleeding from a gash in one of its haunches.

"What happened?" Josiah asked.

"It was that awful New Jersey Devil!" Mrs. Sorbiski cried out. "I let Eustace out to frolic in the yard one last time before we turned in, and this — this *thing* flew down and tried to eat him! It looked like some kind of flying kangaroo! But I beat it with my broom, and then it flew away, the filthy beast!"

"Which way did it go?"

"I don't know! Up!"

With a sigh, Josiah turned Sunlight away, picked a direction, and started riding down the road, hoping to catch sight of the devil.

For an hour, he rode all through Camden, pulling his Henry rifle out of the saddle holster and keeping at the ready, but he found no sign. He cursed the creature's lack of an eldritch origin to keep it from being detected by the Horvath amulet that bounced against his chest as he rode.

It was past midnight when he finally decided to give up and call it a night. First, he had to bring the horse back to the stable. The boarding house had nowhere to house a horse overnight, but Mr. Kawalski had kindly given Josiah a key to the stables so he could return the horse regardless of the lateness of the hour.

His entrance woke the stable boy, who blearily took charge of Sunlight to wipe him down, feed him, and water him before settling the steed down for the night.

Josiah tipped the boy a penny, and also asked that he tell Mr. Kawalski that Josiah would require Sunlight's services the following day, before slinging the Henry rifle over his shoulder and taking his leave, locking the stable door behind him.

He heard the sounds of carousing as he walked down Ferry Avenue toward 7th Street. The Black Hawk Social Club was at that corner, and Josiah knew its members often drank into the night.

Just as he approached the corner, he heard another blood-curdling scream, though this was of a much deeper timbre than that of Mary Sorbiski's.

The door to the saloon flew open, and four men came dashing out.

"Run for your lives!"

"It's the devil himself!"

"I'm sorry, Myrna, I'll never drink again!"

The fourth just screamed, and unlike the others, ran right toward Josiah.

Intercepting him and grabbing him by the shoulders, Josiah saw that the man had bloodshot eyes and his breath stunk of cheap liquor. He hadn't shaved in a few days, but his clothes were of a higher quality than that of your usual drunk. Then again, Mr. Rouh, the proprietor, only let members into the club, and his clientele were generally gentlemen of *some* station.

"What's going on?" Josiah asked the man, who was surprised enough by Josiah accosting him to stop screaming, thank the heavens.

"There's — there's a — a *monster* behind the club! It's the Wozzle Bug, I swear it! Let me go, damn you!"

Josiah did as the man asked, and the drunkard commenced to screaming again and continuing to run down Ferry Avenue. For his part, Josiah ran the other way, going down 7th to the back of the saloon. His Henry rifle had been resting diagonally across his back. As he ran, he slid it over his head and held it in front of his body.

In the alley behind the club, staring into the back window, was a creature unlike any Josiah had ever seen in person, though it did bear at least a certain resemblance to Speelman's drawing.

It stood at about Josiah's own height, perhaps a little shorter. It had skin that seemed like horsehide or leather. A pair of wings of the same consistency protruded from its back. Its fierce snout was filled with sharp teeth, a detail that had been missing from Speelman's sketch. It stood on two legs, and while Josiah couldn't make out its feet in the darkness, its hands — if one could even call them that — were quite clear. The fingers ended in talons that appeared sharper even than the teeth. The creature also had a long tail, the length of which Josiah could not determine in the poor light.

The legs, however, were bent back from the knee very much like that of a kangaroo, which was probably why so many witnesses described it thusly—though it bore little resemblance to that Australian animal otherwise.

Amazingly, the creature hadn't noticed him yet. He needed to take advantage of this to immobilize the creature. Reaching into his coat pocket, he went to pull out the velvet pouch he had obtained from Miss Silverio.

Just as he started to open the pouch, the back door flew open, and the club's proprietor, Mr. Frank Rouh, came bursting out brandishing a large club, screaming even more loudly than the man Josiah had accosted on Ferry Avenue.

The creature's wings spread even as Josiah opened the pouch. Purple smoke filtered into the air, filling the alley, but the creature had already taken to the night sky and was unaffected.

"What in tarnation—?" Rouh turned to face Josiah, still holding the club over his head.

Ignoring him, Josiah cursed, raised his rifle upward, and shot at the fleeing creature. But it was already almost out of sight.

"What in blazes was that flummery?" Rouh cried out, waving his arms back and forth to disperse the purple smoke, but Josiah ignored him and ran down 7th Street.

The Jersey Devil flew in a straight line down 7th, which Josiah considered a kindness. It landed on a rooftop, and Josiah pulled the rifle's lever and shot again.

But the monster took to the air once more before the bullet could strike.

Josiah continued to run, but they were in a part of Camden that was not serviced by the electric streetlamps—indeed, hadn't been serviced even by gas lamps back in the day—and as it was a new moon, nature provided no light of its own.

Still, he ran through the streets, hoping to catch a glimpse, cursing his awful timing once again. He had missed the creature in Haddon Heights by half an hour, and he had the great misfortune to not come across the devil here in Camden until after he'd stabled his horse. Had he been astride Sunlight, he might have been able to keep pace with the monster.

Or at least not lost sight of it.

By this time, it was nearly two in the morning. The creature's ability to fly meant it could go anywhere, and he had no way of tracking it. Worse, he had just wasted his only method of stopping it from taking flight.

It also looked like no creature he had ever seen before, so he could not go back to Miss Silverio or to the Wardein and ask for a talisman to track it, for such talismans were quite specific in their function.

Once again shouldering his rifle, he trudged back toward Mrs. Van Leuwen's boarding house.

The next morning, he got up at dawn's early light, as ever. Mrs. Van Leuwen fed him an excellent breakfast, mercifully alone, as Mr. Pratt had apparently gone to bed at some point.

"I heard," Mrs. Van Leuwen said as she poured his coffee, having already given him wheatcakes topped with butter and maple syrup, "that some men got together in Jacksonville with hounds to try to track down the Wozzle Bug — but the hounds refused to chase it down! Can you believe that?"

To preserve Mrs. Van Leuwen's lack of awareness of Josiah's vocation as a Slayer, he simply shook his head in sympathy. In truth, the hounds wouldn't have been able to pick up the scent of the creature once it took to the air, but only some of the sightings had mentioned the devil's wings.

After breakfast, Josiah stopped by the store to make sure that young Oliver Richardson had opened that morning. In fact, he had, and rolled his eyes at Josiah's entrance. "You don't need to check on me, Jed."

"My apologies, Ollie, but I needed to be sure. Emmy wouldn't let me hear the end of it if she found out I didn't check up on you."

"She's asleep, how would she know?"

"Trust me," Josiah said with a knowing chuckle, "she'd know."

"If you say so. Where are you headed today?"

"Pennsauken, once I collect the horse that I've hired."

Oliver shook his head. "I keep telling you, you should get an automobile. That's how everyone will travel in the future."

"Then in the future is when I'll get one. For now, I have to go to too many places that do not have roadways. I need a conveyance that can go anywhere, not just where there happen to be stone or dirt paths."

Tilting his head and squinting, Oliver said, "If you say so."

"I say so. Take care of the place, please, Ollie."

"Good luck, Jed!"

Josiah then proceeded to Mr. Kawalski's to retrieve Sunlight.

"Didja hear about the ruckus over at the Black Hawk? Men there saw the Jabberwock, and some damn fool nearly shot Mr. Rouh."

Josiah snorted. "I not only heard about it, I was part of it. In fact, I was nearly able to capture the — the Jabberwock."

"You mean the damn fool was you?"

Chuckling, Josiah said, "I'm afraid so. But I was attempting to shoot the Jabberwock, not Mr. Rouh. Had he not come running out the back door like a madman, I might have been able to shoot the creature head-on."

"Pity. I heard they tried to set dogs on it in Hammonton, and the dogs refused to track it."

"You're the second person I've heard say that today," Josiah said with a smirk, "though I heard that it was in Jacksonville."

"Either way, not really like a dog to do that, is it?"

"No," Josiah said, "but having now seen the Jabberwock in person, I can hardly bring myself to blame the hounds for keeping their distance."

"Sunlight seems a little peaked. You rode him pretty hard yesterday."

"I didn't!" Josiah drew himself up straight. "We covered quite a bit of distance." He told Mr. Kawalski of all the places he went the previous day. "I only brought him to a full gallop once, when I heard Mrs. Sorbiski scream."

"Fine, fine," Mr. Kawalski said. "Where do you plan to take him today?"

"Pennsauken, then likely to Philadelphia."

Making a noise like an automobile engine turning over, Mr. Kawalski said, "Be careful with him, all right?"

"Always." Josiah hauled himself up onto Sunlight's saddle and took him out of the stable at an easy trot.

He arrived at Pennsauken in the late morning, heading straight for one of the oldest houses of worship in the county. The First Presbyterian Church had been part of the township since before the Revolutionary War, and its current pastor, the Reverend Ezekiel Grigsby, was not only a childhood friend of Josiah's but had also been a useful contact since he'd become a Slayer. Ezekiel had provided the incantation that removed the foul spirit from the haberdashery in the village of Maple Shade, not to mention his aid in getting rid of a dragon that had menaced several homes in Trenton.

Tying his horse to the hitching post by the trough, Josiah gave Sunlight a good pat on the neck and then went inside the large stone edifice.

Inside, Josiah saw Ezekiel standing by the altar, speaking to a man in a tweed suit.

Josiah stayed by the rear of the church, glancing at the bulletin board — which was covered in signs about various community activities — before Ezekiel called out, "Jed!"

The man in the tweed suit shook Ezekiel's hand and then moved off toward the side exit to the church. Josiah walked down the center aisle between the rows of chairs and approached Ezekiel, who wore a light-colored collarless shirt, a dark waistcoat, and a dark jacket. His curly hair had gone prematurely gray while he was in divinity school, making him appear older than his years — which, in truth, served him well in his vocation.

Offering his hand, and with a very bright smile on his face, Ezekiel said, "Good to see you, Jed. What brings you to our township?"

Josiah accepted the handshake, but then Ezekiel pulled him into an embrace. Patting him on the back after recovering from the surprise, he said, "Always a pleasure, Zeke. And I'm afraid I'm here on business."

They broke the embrace, and now the smile had been replaced by a most serious expression. Ezekiel knew full well that Josiah's business often involved danger. "I'm sorry to hear that."

"Are you familiar with the so-called Jersey Devil that has been menacing the area of late?"

Ezekiel scoffed. "I've heard stories, yes. They all sound like purest poppycock. Some of the farmers got together to hunt this mythical beast just the other day."

Wincing, Josiah said, "I'm afraid it's not poppycock, old friend. I saw the creature myself last night in Camden. And it's those very farmers that I'm here about."

"So, you wish me to introduce them to you?"

That brought Josiah up short. "I had been told that they'd gone missing. That they searched for the Jersey Devil and never returned."

After throwing his head back and laughing so hard, it echoed throughout the large structure, Ezekiel said, "What fathead told you such a thing? No, they went out at noontime, then came back after sunset without having found a thing."

"It seems I made a mistake in trusting the accounts of the newspapers."

"Ah, yes, that was obviously your first mistake."

Josiah shook his head. "Truly, I had not trusted them in the first place, believing the entire affair to be an elaborate hoax. But then I *saw* it." He let out a very long breath. "And I therefore made the mistake of thinking that the newspapers had suddenly become bastions of veracity, an error I will not make again."

"Very wise, old friend. Why don't we share a repast? I have some fresh chicken parts that I was going to roast for dinner tonight, but I'd be happy to cook it for lunch instead, and we can catch up."

Josiah hesitated, tempted by the offer. "I'm afraid I cannot, Zeke. If the posse that went after the Devil is not missing, then my reasons for coming here are no longer valid." He considered. "Having said that, before I move on to another town where the Devil was sighted, it might be wise to speak to some of them to learn what they *did* see."

"All right. One of the two who led the expedition was one of my congregants, Benjamin Osler. I can take you to him. The other—" Ezekiel shuddered. "He's a Catholic. I fear you would not get a proper account from a papist any more that you would from a reporter."

"Understood," Josiah said, though he didn't understand at all. Then again, his time as a Slayer had removed pretty much every vestige of his Christian faith. He still believed in the general underlying philosophy espoused by Jesus Christ in the Bible, and in the morality behind church teachings, but he had seen far too much to believe that a benevolent god and his savior offspring truly existed.

But he saw no reason to alienate his oldest friend by saying so to his face.

"Come, it's a short walk to the Osler farm. And Mrs. Osler always puts out a huge lunch for the farmhands—I'm sure we could partake as well."

Josiah chuckled. "And you still have your chicken parts for supper."

"Indeed."

Ezekiel put on an overcoat that Josiah thought would be inadequate to protect the reverend from the cold, but he showed no signs of being chilled when they went outside.

Josiah led Sunlight as they proceeded through Pennsauken to the farms on the outskirts. Ezekiel caught Josiah up on the doings of his church, and also how his parents fared in their move to New York City after his father took a position with Chemical Bank. Josiah, meanwhile, told Ezekiel how Emmelina and the store were doing. He even mentioned the reward for the capture of the

Jersey Devil and what it would mean to be able to finally build a second story.

"That would be a sight to see," Ezekiel said, "an expanded Clevenger's Dry Goods. I suspect your father would turn over in his grave to see the place changed in any way, but your mother would probably be glad to have the store expanded and the two of you under the same roof."

Josiah chuckled. "No doubt."

They approached a farmhouse, behind which was several acres of snow-covered farmland, as well as a tall silo and a stable.

Josiah waited on the street while Ezekiel went down the walkway, up the two steps to the front patio, and then knocked on the door.

A woman answered the door and greeted Ezekiel warmly, giving him a hug. Josiah couldn't make out their conversation, but then Ezekiel walked back to him at the street.

"Come, Jed, I'll lead you to where you can put the horse. Their stable boy will care for him while we join Mr. and Mrs. Osler. As I suspected, they are about to sit down to lunch, and we are welcome to partake."

"Good."

To Josiah's surprise, Ezekiel led him, not to the stable but to the silo. As they got closer, he saw why: something had left a rather large hole in the roof of the stable.

He put the Henry rifle in the saddle holster—it didn't do to bring a weapon to the lunch table—and left Sunlight in the capable care of the stable hands. Ezekiel then brought Josiah to the back door, which led right into the kitchen. The woman from the front door was putting four place settings down on a table in the center of the kitchen. Josiah heard a susurrus of noise coming from another room.

"That's the dining room," Ezekiel said. "The farmhands all eat in there."

"We, however," the woman said, "will eat in here, so we can talk in private—and, more to the point, in quiet."

Ezekiel spoke formally. "Mr. Josiah Clevenger, this is Mrs. Benjamin Osler."

Mrs. Osler gave Ezekiel a murderous look. "Oh, sweet mercy, Reverend, it's Claire."

Josiah grinned. "And I'm Jed. It's a pleasure to meet you, ma'am."

"I say again, it's Claire, Jed. I won't have any formality in my house. Now when we're in church, that's a whole 'nother thing, but that's God's house, and we will show proper respect there. But this is home and hearth, and I find all that formality to be exhausting. So, I'm Claire, and you're Jed, and my husband is Ben."

"And Zeke here is 'Reverend'?" Josiah asked playfully.

"You may call him by his Christian name if you wish, Jed, but he is still a man of God, and I prefer not to be struck down for blasphemy." She finished putting the silverware down, added a pitcher filled with water to the center of the table, and then indicated the chairs. "Well, don't just stand there in your coats, take those things off and give them here, I'll hang them in the closet."

Josiah shrugged out of his wool coat and placed the scarf inside one of the sleeves. He then removed his hat and handed both hat and coat to Claire. Ezekiel likewise removed his overcoat and gave it over as well.

"Thank you," she said with a nod. "Have a seat, both of you. I'll be right back with lunch."

She headed toward the dining room. Josiah took a seat at the table, with Ezekiel sitting opposite him.

Glancing at the door Claire just went through, Josiah said, "She's a fascinating woman."

Before Ezekiel could reply, a deep voice said, "Yes, she is, and I love her for it."

Turning, Josiah saw an immensely tall man with broad shoulders and short brown hair enter through the same back door he and Ezekiel had come through. He immediately sat at one of the chairs perpendicular to Josiah on his left.

"Good to see you, Reverend."

"Likewise, Ben. This is my friend Josiah Clevenger."

Offering his hand, Josiah said, "Good to meet you, Ben. Please, call me Jed."

Benjamin grinned a broad, gap-toothed smile as he accepted Josiah's handshake. "Ah, I see you've already received an earful from my wife on the subject of how we address each other in her house."

"Indeed, we have."

"So, what brings you to our home? I assume it's private business, since Claire has exiled us to the kitchen?"

"I'm afraid so," Ezekiel said. "Jed here is on the trail of the Jersey Devil that you chased after yesterday."

Benjamin gave Josiah a vaguely respectful look, likely believing that Josiah was a bounty hunter. He had led people to believe that as his vocation nearly as often as he did that of a Pinkerton.

Before Benjamin could speak on the subject, however, Claire came in from the dining room, carrying a serving platter filled with sandwiches. Josiah couldn't make out what the meat was between the slices of bread, not that it mattered. "Oh, sweet mercy, would that be the same Jersey Devil that you swore was stuff and nonsense, Reverend?"

Benjamin's grin widened. "And that you said we were fools to be chasing after?"

Ezekiel took the rebuke with a bow of his head. "I may have spoken in error."

Claire put the platter down in the center of the kitchen table, and Josiah could now identify the meat as some manner of pork. As he reached for one of the sandwiches, he said, "I have seen the creature myself, last night in Camden. I had heard that the posse you led had never returned from your expedition, which was why I made Pennsauken my next stop in my pursuit of the Devil. It was the first report of people gone missing."

With a small laugh, Benjamin said, "Nobody went missing. I mean, there was a moment when we thought we lost young Tobias Michaelson, but he was just relieving himself behind a tree. And I'm afraid that was as exciting as the expedition got."

Josiah barely registered Benjamin's words, as he was too busy enjoying the sandwich. "This is delicious," he said before he'd even finished the first bite.

"Thank you."

Swallowing, Josiah then asked, "What led you to mount the expedition?"

"You mean who saw the beast?" Benjamin asked. "We both did."

"Creature straight from hell, it was," Claire said with a shudder. "It went after the pigs."

"In winter, we keep the chickens, the goats, and the pigs in the silo where it's warmer," Benjamin said. "Since the storm, we've also kept the horses in there, since the roof of the stable collapsed from the snow."

"Yes, my own horse was stabled there when we arrived," Josiah said.

Benjamin nodded. "It was time for the animals to get their morning meal, and the farmhands were all busy working on repairing the stable roof or out running errands, so Claire and I took care of the feeding."

Claire picked up the story, giving Benjamin a chance to bite into his own sandwich. "We walked into the silo, and there it was, reaching for one of the goats. It looked like a demon, with horns on its head and those awful wings, and knives at the ends of its fingers."

Josiah nodded. He recalled no horns on the Devil he saw the previous night, but its tapered ears could easily be mistaken for such.

"My shotgun was back in the house," Benjamin said, "but there were some shovels in the silo, so I grabbed one of them."

"What was strange," Claire said after swallowing, "was that it was lurching back and forth, like some kind of — well, someone quite taken with drink."

Josiah recognized the tone of disdain in Claire's voice. She was obviously at least sympathetic to the growing temperance movement, if not an actual member of that group dedicated to eradicating alcohol from human existence.

Benjamin dabbed his mouth with a napkin. "I came at it with the shovel, but it stumbled out of the way, then took to the air and headed back out the door. I gave chase, of course, but it was high in the sky by the time I got outside myself. It flew the way it walked, like a drunkard."

Chewing thoughtfully on the final bite of his sandwich, which he had pretty much devoured while the couple told their story, Josiah compared this to his own experience last night and was disturbed by the differences in the creature's behavior.

"Once I lost sight of it, I immediately gathered up all our farmhands and folks from the other farms nearby. We met outside the church."

"Much," Ezekiel said ruefully, "to my chagrin and complaint."

Claire patted Ezekiel's hand. "We forgive you, Reverend."

Benjamin chuckled. "By lunchtime, we'd assembled a posse, but we searched all afternoon and into sunset, and found no sign of it." He put a finger to his chin. "Come to think on it, I remember a young man at the church I'd never seen before, and he was writing in a notebook."

Ezekiel straightened and almost choked on his sandwich. He coughed for a second, then asked, "What did he look like?"

"Um, he was very short—"

"Oh, sweet mercy, Ben, everyone's short to you." Claire turned to Ezekiel. "He was about your height, Reverend, with a thick red beard and curly brown hair. He wore a leather coat over a brown suit and no hat."

Closing his eyes and letting out a hiss, Ezekiel said, "I should have realized." He opened his eyes and looked at Josiah. "Jed, that young man is why you're here. He was a reporter and was asking around town about the Leeds Devil. I sent him on his way and told him not to bother the good people of our town with his nonsense. I saw him later at the telegraph office, no doubt providing the very story you read about the Pennsauken posse going missing."

"What time was he at the telegraph office?" Claire asked.

Ezekiel thought a moment. "Around four in the afternoon."

"They hadn't come back yet," Claire said, "and they'd only been out a few hours. What a chowderhead that man is."

"To be fair," Josiah said, pouring himself some water from the pitcher, "he may have telegraphed in only that they were still out and hadn't returned, and the newspaper editors may have decided to sensationalize the story. Trust me, it would *not* be the first time."

"I will say," Benjamin added, "that we did see some odd tracks that looked like an unshod horse, but it could very easily have been just that. Still, not many horses go without shoes around here. It could've been the Jersey Devil, but we never saw it before it got dark. And it's a new moon, so..."

"Besides which," Josiah said with a smile, "I know from personal experience that it was in Camden last night. It attacked a dog and frightened the members of a social club."

"It can fly, though I can't imagine its ability to navigate is anything to write home about," Benjamin said.

"True."

The Oslers had little else to say about the Jersey Devil, and the conversation soon moved to various bits of town gossip that Josiah knew or cared very little about, though he pretended to be interested for Ezekiel's sake.

Propriety kept him from leaving before the meal was formally over, but as soon as it was, he stood up and said, "My apologies, Ben, Claire, but I must take my leave with dispatch. This information has been valuable, but I need to move on."

"To where?"

"The creature seems to be moving westward—Pemberton, Haddon Heights, here, Camden. I suspect it might cross the Delaware into Pennsylvania, so I'm going there next."

"Well, good luck to you, Jed," Claire said. "Would you like to take a sandwich with you?"

Josiah agreed wholeheartedly with that notion, and Claire went ahead and wrapped two of her sandwiches in paper for him and gave them to him with his coat, scarf, and hat.

Ezekiel walked him out to the silo.

"Thank you, Zeke. This has been a help." He smiled wryly. "Not sure how yet, but every piece of information is useful, given that this is a new creature."

That got a wide-eyed expression from Ezekiel. "This isn't a beast you've encountered before?"

Shaking his head, Josiah said, "I'm afraid not. That's troubling, only insofar as that means I've no idea how to stop the thing." He patted the saddle holster for his rifle. "Worst case, I always have this."

Josiah walked Sunlight out of the silo, tipping his hat to the stable hand as he went, and then hoisted himself into the saddle.

"God be with you, Jed," Ezekiel said. "I hope you catch this thing quickly. And not just so you can get that $10,000 reward."

"Thank you, Zeke. I'll send word once I've solved the case."

"I'd appreciate that." Ezekiel grinned. "I hate not knowing the end of the story. It's why I took to the clergy — the Bible provides the ending to every story in the Book of Revelation."

Josiah shook his head and chuckled. "Be well, Zeke."

With that, he rode southwest, heading back home to Camden. His next stop was going to be Philadelphia, but he didn't wish to subject Sunlight to the big city, plus getting the horse across on a ferry would be more expensive than going on his own. He would probably make use of a hansom cab while in the City of Brotherly Love, which would also be expensive. However, he could also add the cost of it to his invoice for Grimwade.

He worked his way down River Avenue, enjoying the view it provided of the Delaware. The wind off the water was quite cold, but for some reason, today, he found it invigorating rather than chilling.

And then he saw it.

The Jersey Devil that he saw last night, flying lazily and awkwardly through the air.

The creature flew down toward the ground just short of the river. There was an expanse of grass and trees between River Avenue and the shoreline in this spot. Josiah turned Sunlight to the right and kicked him into a slow gallop.

The Jersey Devil looped around into a landing by the river. It showed none of the grace and speed it had displayed when flying away from the Black Hawk the previous night.

"Hyah!" Josiah cried, now urging Sunlight into a full gallop while also pulling his rifle out from its saddle holster.

The creature stood by the river, leaning into it and drinking from the water. Josiah tugged on the reins with his left hand to bring Sunlight to a halt, then levered a silver bullet into the rifle's chamber and went to aim. The stock rested comfortably on the soft spot under his right clavicle. The skin there was rough and calloused from multiple uses of the rifle. He pointed the long barrel directly at the Jersey Devil.

The creature had ignored Sunlight's hoofbeats on the grassy ground, but at the metallic clack of the rifle being made ready to shoot, the creature stopped drinking from the Delaware River and looked straight at Josiah.

And then the Slayer realized something was wrong.

True, he last saw the creature at night, lit only by the street-lamps, and now he saw it in daylight, albeit on a winter day that was gray and overcast.

But it still looked *different* somehow.

Its skin seemed more wrinkled, for one thing, though he supposed that could've been the difference in lighting. The talons on its hands seemed longer and sharper—and thinner, too. The wings seemed wider, as well.

But the biggest difference, the one thing he could not discount as a trick of the light, was the eyes.

The eyes of the Jersey Devil he encountered behind the Black Hawk Social Club had been cold, hard, calculating.

The eyes of the creature that stood before him now on the banks of the Delaware River were none of those things. They were wild, unfocused, unsure.

In his confusion, Josiah hesitated.

In that hesitation, the Devil took to the air.

Cursing, Josiah shot at the creature, but it was already well past the point he aimed at by the time the bullet reached that spot. He levered in another round but couldn't take aim. Unlike last night, the creature flew in a haphazard manner, bucking and weaving—

—like a drunkard.

Cursing again, he tried to figure out what course the Devil was flying on, but it soon went out of sight, its path so erratic that any theory as to where it was going would be pure guesswork.

But now, he also had to face the possibility, first conceived when he'd heard the story told by Mr. Speelman's cook, that there were *two* of these beasts roaming the countryside.

He continued on his way back to Camden, as his need to be in Philadelphia as soon as possible had increased.

The trip into town was eerily quiet, as there were very few people on the streets. Word of the events of the previous night with Mrs. Sorbiski and at the Black Hawk had apparently spread. Normally, the late afternoon thoroughfares would be filled with people, but he saw very few souls.

He returned Sunlight to the stable, which was closed uncharacteristically early. Luckily, Josiah still had the padlock key. The stable boy remained on duty, wide awake this time, and he took care of Sunlight.

Next, Josiah went to the store, where Emmelina sat behind the counter, reading a book.

She looked up excitedly when Josiah entered, only to deflate when she got a good look at him. "Oh, it's only you."

"Good to see you, as well, Emmy."

"Oh, don't be an ass, Jed." She stood up. "You're the first person to walk through that door since I relieved Oliver at noontime. Everyone is frightened of that ridiculous beast. And what are you doing here, anyhow? Shouldn't you be out catching it?"

"I believe it's in Philadelphia right now. I just left the horse with Mr. Kawalski, and I'm about to go to the ferry, but I wished to check in with you first to make sure you're all right."

Emmelina rolled her eyes. "I'm a grown woman of five and thirty years, Jed. I hardly need you to nursemaid me." She waved her arms in a shooing gesture. "Now get moving to Philadelphia already and capture that beast!"

Wrapping his scarf around his neck, Josiah silently turned and left the store.

The river ferry was as empty as he'd ever seen as it made its journey. On the water, the wind was an even more bitter cold than it had been on the shore, and he no longer found it bracing.

He recalled reading of President Washington's trip across this river, sailing to Trenton from the Pennsylvania side on Christmas night in 1776. The sun was starting to set for Josiah's crossing, while Washington had gone the other way in the middle of the night, albeit with a full moon to light the way.

Josiah felt his hands go numb from the cold.

As he disembarked from the ferry on the Philadelphia side, he heard two boys arguing.

"The Leeds Devil is at the Taggart School right now! I heard all about it!"

"No, it's not, my friend Martin told me it was flying out toward Chester!"

A man walked up to separate the boys before their argument came to blows. "Boys, quit your yammering! It cannot be at the Taggart School any longer, for they chased it away after they closed the school for the day. Now move along."

Josiah thought about what he'd heard. He could try going to the Taggart School, see if there was any hint to the Devil's whereabouts.

But Chester was, at least in a general sense, in the same direction that the Devil had flown away from Josiah, so it might—*might*—have been the creature's destination.

It wasn't much to go on, but he had, in truth, very little else. The creature—or creatures, since it more and more seemed likely there were two—was moving in a vaguely southwesterly direction, but there seemed to be little rhyme or reason, beyond attacking livestock of various sorts.

If nothing else, there were farms in Chester, which seemed to be where the creature liked to find animals. Though not exclusively, either, especially given the way it had menaced people in Camden and Haddon Heights.

Deciding he had nothing to lose and no preferable alternative, he went in search of a hansom cab that would take him to Chester.

The cab's horses trotted through the thoroughfares of Philadelphia, periodically passed by single horses and the occasional automobile. Josiah found himself musing on what improvements they could make to the store with $10,000—and even more, if he could convince the zoo that two Jersey Devils would be worth paying $20,000. He might even be willing to negotiate for $15,000.

While Philadelphia had far more people walking the snow-covered streets than Camden did, it still felt more subdued than usual, and what people were out seemed to be huddling together and looking around more.

In particular, people were looking *up* a great deal. As if they expected the Jersey Devil to swoop down out of the sky and snatch them away.

The cab moved out of the city, continuing on a road that ran parallel to the railroad tracks. Which was fitting, as the specific destination he had given the cab driver was the train station in Chester. It seemed the best place to start.

As they ambled down the roadway, Josiah saw a freight train sitting idle on the tracks.

And then he caught sight of two young women who were screaming and running away from the train.

Using the stock of his rifle, Josiah tapped the ceiling of the cab. "Stop here, driver!" he cried out.

With a loud "Whoa!" the driver brought the horses to a halt.

Once the carriage had stopped, Josiah hopped out of the cab and signaled the two girls, one a tall, thin blonde, the other a short, stout brunette.

"Help us, please!"

"What is it?" Josiah asked as they ran toward him.

"We saw it!" the blonde screamed.

The brunette cried out, "The Leeds Devil!"

"Where?" Josiah asked urgently.

The blonde pointed at the freight train. "In the boxcar over there!"

Josiah followed her finger to see that there was an open boxcar on the train and some kind of figure in it. It was too far away to make it out, though—for all he knew, it was a hobo, and the girls had a vivid imagination.

Then he turned to the girls and frowned at them. "What were you doing here unattended?"

The girls exchanged furtive glances. "We—we like to watch the trains go by," the blonde one said nervously.

Sticking her chin out defiantly, the brunette said, "We're sixteen. We don't *need* chaperones, thank you very much."

Josiah doubted that, somehow, but he wasn't in a position to deal with these two girls being out on their own without adult supervision.

Instead, he stuck with what he *was* in a position to deal with. "Are you sure it was the Leeds Devil?"

"What else could it have been?" the blonde asked.

The brunette added, "It looked like an alligator crossed with an opossum—but with wings!"

"And it snarled at us," the blonde put in.

"All right, come with me." He led the girls to the cab. Reaching into his pocket, he pulled out a couple of greenbacks and handed them to the driver. "These girls need to stay safe in the cab while I investigate that train over there."

The driver had accepted the cash handily but now was looking apprehensively at the train. "I do not understand."

"Just let them stay here with you. I'll be back soon."

"What if you're not?" the driver asked.

Josiah considered that. "If I'm not back in half an hour—or if you see something happen to me from here—then take these girls wherever they need to go." He handed the driver the full fare for the trip to Chester, which he was originally going to pay upon arriving at that destination, and then added an additional five dollars.

Hastily pocketing the cash, the driver said, "As you say, sir. Good luck."

"Thank you." He turned to the girls. "Wait here in the cab."

The brunette started to say, "We can take care of ours—"

But the blonde interrupted. "Thank you, sir."

Nodding, Josiah left the girls in the cab driver's care and started to move toward the freight train, pausing only to lever a round into the chamber of his rifle.

He walked at a quick pace, both hands on the rifle. At present, he pointed the barrel down toward the ground, but it would be the act of less than a second to raise it and pull the trigger. His right hand gripped the stock firmly, forefinger by the trigger.

With the sun setting in the west, there was insufficient illumination to see the figure standing in the open boxcar, but as he grew closer, Josiah could at least make out the general shape. It was a biped for sure, but it could as easily have been a man as his quarry. He couldn't verify the presence of wings, but as yet, he could not verify their absence, either.

Then, as he got ever closer, he finally got a good look at the figure's legs, and they bent back at the knee, just like the Jersey Devil.

Emboldened, Josiah started to jog toward the boxcar. The creature was in a slumped position—indeed, were it not for the odd leg shape and the increasingly obvious lack of clothes, he might have mistaken it at first glance for a sleeping hobo—but Josiah didn't wish to risk the Devil flying away from him a third time.

Once he was about ten yards from the boxcar, he stopped and held up his rifle, pointing it at the creature's head.

It was definitely the same one he encountered on the banks of the Delaware on the road from Pennsauken to Camden.

He said, "Do *not* move!"

The Devil looked up, and Josiah saw the same wildness, the same unfocused madness that was there earlier in the day.

But he saw something else, as well: fatigue. The Jersey Devil was *tired*.

What's more, as it lay slumped in the boxcar, Josiah thought it looked incredibly *old*.

Then Josiah was startled by a keening wail from above and behind him. Whirling around, he saw *another* Jersey Devil swooping down from the sky right at him.

He dove to the ground, somehow managing to keep his grip on the rifle, barely avoiding being on the receiving end of the creature's talons.

As he got to his feet, he saw the second Devil land. He gripped the rifle in both hands again but kept it lowered for the nonce.

In a voice that sounded like broken glass, the Devil said, "Take your leave, now, human, or suffer the consequences."

That brought Josiah up short. "You can speak!"

"Of course, I can speak!"

"You weren't especially talkative last night at the social club in Camden."

"Nor were you — you simply tried to shoot me. If you raise that rifle again, you will not survive long enough to pull the trigger."

Not that he required the verification, but now Josiah knew for sure that this second creature was the one he had encountered in Camden the night before. He was also grateful he had had the instinct to keep the rifle lowered until he could get a sense of what was going on.

A sense he didn't truly have yet.

The creature continued: "I have been searching for my father for the better part of a week. I simply wish to bring him home. Give us leave to do so, and you will not hear from us again."

"I have heard of nothing *but* you—well, the pair of you—for that very week-long span you just cited. The entire Delaware Valley is awash with stories of the Jersey Devil."

The Devil scoffed. "Is that what they call us now? Humans..." The creature shook its head.

"Because of these sightings, I was hired to stop you." Josiah hesitated. He didn't normally introduce himself to his prey, but his prey was rarely this eloquent. And those that were generally declared their impure intentions openly. They certainly never claimed anything as beneficent as rescuing their fathers...

And so, he said, "My name is Josiah Clevenger. I'm a Slayer."

"I gathered as much. We have encountered your kind in the past."

The use of the plural pronoun prompted another question. "How many of you are there?"

"At present, only the two of us, and I fear my father will not be with us much longer." The creature straightened. "I am called Quinque Tredecim. My father is Quattuor Tredecim. He is—is quite old and losing his faculties. A week ago, he left our home in the night, and I have spent the time since attempting to locate him. Now that I have succeeded, at last, I will *not* let anyone stop me, Slayer—not you, not anyone."

Josiah stood his ground, not sure what to do. He couldn't simply let these creatures go—but he wasn't entirely sure he'd be able to stop one of them, much less two.

Then he heard a weak, papery whisper come from the boxcar.

"Quinque? Is—is that you, my daughter?"

Another in a series of surprises for Josiah: the younger Jersey Devil was female.

Quinque turned to face her father. "Yes, Father, I'm here. I'm going to take you back to the cabin."

"You have a cabin?"

Turning back to face Josiah, Quinque said, "Yes. If I take you there and show you that we mean no harm to anyone, will you leave us be and allow my father to die in peace?"

"I—"

"You may rest assured, Mr. Clevenger, that you will not see hide nor hair of either of us again after today. I will make sure my father and I stay hidden. I give you my word."

"You do?"

"Yes."

"And of what value is the word of a creature such as yourself?"

Quinque opened her arms wide. "In the last week, have you seen any real harm done to anyone by my father or myself?"

"I have seen harm done to livestock."

Waving a taloned hand back and forth, Quinque said, "Yes, because Father was hungry. But he was only interested in food, and you can hardly fault him for that. Or do you also hunt people who breed cows and pigs?"

"Of course not."

"Then I ask again, Mr. Clevenger, have you seen any real harm done to anyone by my father or myself?"

Josiah hesitated and then was forced to admit: "I have not."

"Then I would ask that you take me at my word. We none of us have done any harm to anyone."

That phrasing caught Josiah's attention, and he started to lift the rifle slightly. "'We none of us'? You said that you were the only two of your kind."

"You have not answered my question, Mr. Clevenger. Will you accompany us back to our cabin? Once there, you will see that what I say is true."

Josiah's brain swam with confusion. This was not how he had expected his confrontation with the Jersey Devil to go.

So, he answered her question with a question of his own: "Where is this cabin?"

"In the Pine Barrens."

Wincing, Josiah said, "That is fifty miles from here."

"It won't take us long to get there."

"It might not take *you* long to get there, but you may observe that I am not equipped with wings."

"Yes, but we are," Quinque said, and then without another word, she lunged and grabbed Josiah by the shoulders.

The next thing he knew, he was being taken into the air, wind whipping into his face and blowing his hat off. He barely managed to hang onto his rifle.

As they rose from the ground, Josiah found himself thinking that he hadn't actually agreed to come along—but he also wasn't in a position to refuse to go at this point.

He found himself completely taken with the amazing view of eastern Pennsylvania he suddenly had. It was like looking at a map rather than the real world.

Dimly, he registered that the father—was his name Quattuor?—was lazily flying behind Quinque. They headed northward along the Delaware, and soon he saw Philadelphia on one side of the river and his home of Camden on the other before they started to move eastward.

Josiah had so much he wanted to say, but he found himself unable to speak. For one thing, it was very *loud* up here in the air, with the wind constantly blowing in his face and sounding loudly in his ears.

And then, finally, when they were over the wasteland of the Pine Barrens, the ground started to grow closer, and for a moment, Josiah was terrified that he was about to die, smashed to a pulp below.

But no, they slowed and landed softly.

For several seconds, he just stood there. He'd read about the Wright brothers and their aeroplane, but he never imagined he would be able to take to the air himself.

Quattuor landed next to them almost a full minute later. Josiah still found that he could not make his legs move.

Quinque walked up to the older creature. "Are you all right, Father?"

"I need to sleep."

"Go inside. Avram will take care of you."

It wasn't until Quattuor walked slowly toward it that Josiah truly registered that they stood just outside a very large log cabin.

It was three stories tall, plus what looked like a small attic space, and it was as wide as Mrs. Van Leuwen's boarding house. Quattuor opened the front door and went inside. Josiah saw movement but couldn't make out any particular figures. That certainly helped explain Quinque's use of "we none of us," but it was also still at odds with her insistence that she and her father were the only Jersey Devils.

Josiah finally found his voice. "That—that—that was—"

"My apologies, Mr. Clevenger," Quinque said. "But your equivocations grew tiresome, and I did not wish to remain there much longer, lest the railroad authorities decided to investigate."

"I—I—" He cleared his throat. "I did rather like that hat."

Josiah found he couldn't read the facial expression Quinque gave in response to that, but it was probably a disdainful one.

Rather than reply verbally, Quinque instead indicated the front door. "Before I bring you inside, I must ask that you place your rifle down outside. I will have no violence in my house."

"Why do you think there will be violence?"

"Because you are a Slayer."

Josiah considered. Then he walked to the wall next to the front door and placed the rife down, but upright, the stock on the ground, the barrel leaning against the wall.

"I will commit no acts of violence in your house, Miss Tredecim. I give you my word."

"I hope I can trust your word, Mr. Clevenger," Quinque said.

"As I hope that I can trust yours."

With that, Quinque opened the door.

It opened to a wide area, with a balcony on the perimeter of the space on the second floor.

Inside, he saw a sea monster, a lizard man, a jackalope, and two giant monkeys—as well as a being he recognized.

"Sokanon?"

The Thunderbird in question stood near the fireplace that was opposite the front door. She looked up with her owl-like face. Seeing Josiah, she spread her wings and rose into the air. Her entire body seemed as if it were made of living wood, including the wings that brought her aloft.

A sound of thunder rumbled in the distance.

"I'm not going back!" Sokanon's voice echoed as if she had been yelling into an empty barrel.

Quinque let out a hiss. "Sokanon, no! Mr. Clevenger is not here for you, and he has promised to commit no act of violence while here. A promise he made because *I* assured him that no one in this house would harm anyone. If you make a liar of me, then you will be cast out of this place forevermore."

Sokanon had been glaring menacingly at Josiah, but at Quinque's words, she softened—if her obsidian face could ever be said to soften—and returned to the floor.

"I take it," Josiah said slowly, "that Sokanon is here seeking asylum from the Algonquins?"

"Yes," Quinque said. "She does not wish to serve the tribe but wishes simply to—"

Nodding, Josiah finished the sentence. "To live her own life, yes. Her tribe hired me to find her the last time she ran away. She told me how she felt, but I was obligated to fulfill the client's wishes." He looked at Sokanon. "However, as Miss Tredecim said, I am not here for you now, Sokanon, and I fulfilled the Tribal Council's commission when I brought you back four years ago."

"Why are you here, then?"

"To stop us," Quattuor said dolefully. He was sitting in a large chair, being attended to by one of the giant monkeys, presumably Avram.

"Yes, well, Father, if you hadn't gone wandering and menacing the populace, Mr. Clevenger here wouldn't have been hired to stop you, now, would he?"

"I am sorry, Quinque. I—I lost my head."

"You almost did so literally."

Josiah looked around. In addition to the creatures he'd seen upon entering, there was also a giant bat that flew across the balcony.

"What *is* this place?" he asked.

The lizard man stepped forward, his narrow feet making a squishing noise on the wooden floor. "A place your fellow Slayers must never learn of," he said. "Even now, I do not trust that you will not try to slaughter us all."

"He will not," Quinque said.

"I appreciate the testimonial," Josiah said dryly.

Quinque actually smiled at that. Or, at the very least, bared her teeth. "It was no such thing, Mr. Clevenger, simply a statement that, should you attempt to do so, you will fail, and then you will die."

"You told me you have never harmed anyone."

"We haven't—yet. The only circumstance under which I would allow it is to defend ourselves."

The lizard man's tongue flicked out like that of a frog. "We will not strike the first blow, Slayer—but rest assured that we would strike the last."

Josiah swallowed. Avoiding the murderous gaze of the lizard man, he regarded Quinque with curiosity. "How did this place come about?"

"That is a tale of some length. Why don't you sit yourself down? Saltadora, please fetch our guest a cup of tea."

The giant monkey that wasn't caring for Quattuor nodded and loped off toward the spiral staircase, then walked around it. Presumably, the kitchen was back that way.

Josiah appreciated the offer to sit, as his impromptu flight had left him unsteady on his feet, but he also feared the very idea of being anywhere but standing in front of the door. However, he decided that he needed to trust Quinque.

Besides, she was right about one thing. Even if he'd had his rifle on his person, he wouldn't stand a chance by himself against *all* these monsters.

So the wisest recourse would be to sit in one of the chairs, wait for Saltadora to bring him tea, enjoy the warmth of the fireplace, and listen to Quinque tell her story.

"It began almost two centuries ago at what is now known as Leeds Point, specifically with a Quaker family..."

Chapter Three

Deborah Smith Leeds screamed from the pain that suffused her entire body, her cries louder even than the thunder that exploded outside the Leeds home as rain pelted down against the house's wooden frame.

She had given birth a dozen times before. All twelve children had survived, as had she, which she knew made her entire family more blessed than most. Many a stillborn child had been buried in the township since Deborah had arrived from England to marry Japheth Leeds fifteen years ago. And many grave markers told of women who'd died during the birthing process.

Yet despite having gone through it so often, despite the pain being spectacularly horrible every single time, she was still on each occasion caught off guard by how agonizing the process was.

Once, after their fifth child was born, Japheth had asked her what the pain was like. After considering it for several seconds, she finally settled on replying thusly: "Take your lip's bottom and pull it entirely over your head."

That was, she knew, an inadequate response, but she had no other analogue that Japheth would comprehend. The only pain that came even close was the crampings that came each month with her courses, but Japheth never truly understood *that* pain, either.

Deborah sat on her birthing stool, screaming in pain, only occasionally opening her eyes to see her older cousin Elisabeth, acting as midwife, sitting on her own stool facing Deborah's open legs.

"Almost there, Mother Leeds," she said. "Just hold on."

Her only reply to that was another scream.

"Here it comes!" Elisabeth cried out.

Only then did Deborah notice that the midwife's arms were covered in blood.

The next thing Deborah knew, the pain was gone. It had always been this way: one moment, a hurt so awful that Deborah was convinced she would not survive, and the very next moment, no pain at all.

But though the pain was gone, the exhaustion was, as ever, almost overwhelming. It took all of Deborah's efforts to not fall asleep in the birthing stool.

And then she realized what she wasn't hearing. The thunder still cracked periodically, and the rain still steadily hammered against the house.

But she heard no sounds from the babe.

Elisabeth looked stricken, bowing her gray head. "I'm—I'm sorry, Mother Leeds, but—"

Deborah closed her eyes, tears welling in them. "The child is dead?" she asked bluntly, not wishing to hear her cousin equivocate.

"Yes. I'm sorry."

Opening her eyes, Deborah shifted position so she could sit more comfortably, no longer needing to keep her legs apart. "You've nothing to apologize for, Elisabeth. It's my own fault."

Now Elisabeth looked even more stricken, which Deborah would not have thought possible a moment previous. "Oh, no, don't say that!"

"It's true." She wiped the tears from her eyes and cheeks. "If you recall, I learned I was with this child last autumn, right after the millwright terminated Japheth's employment."

"Yes'm," Elisabeth said quietly as she gently wrapped the stillborn child in a blanket and placed it in the basket next to her.

"At the time, I was furious and exhausted and angry. And I cursed to the heavens and made a most unfortunate oath."

"I understand."

Deborah was glad that her cousin did comprehend the reality, for she did not wish to repeat the oath in any way.

Japheth had been drowning in wine that night. In fact, he had been drowning in wine most nights, which was why the millwright had refused to continue to employ him, even though he was in need of able-bodied men to construct a new flour mill in the Pine Barrens.

And then Deborah had cursed to heaven and cried out in anguish that she did not wish to have a thirteenth child, that the devil should take it from her. She was barely able to put food on the table with the money she made from selling the healing herbs she grew in their garden, as well as the recipes for using them properly. Their oldest son, Joshua, was working for the Fothergills on their farm, which brought some money to the household. Their oldest daughter, Junia, had become apprentice to Margery Savery, the local seamstress, but that would not result in paying work for another year. The other children were still too young to work—indeed, Junia was younger than most apprentices, but Margery had said that Junia was more skilled than girls three years older. Still, Japheth *needed* to be working as well.

And the millwright was not the first person to terminate Japheth's employment due to his predilection for drink.

Still, Deborah's exhortation to the Almighty had been foolish, and she was now convinced that God had punished her for her expression of repugnance for bringing another child into the world.

And this poor, innocent soul had died for her hubris.

Japheth came into the bedroom, then. "Oh, thank heavens," he said upon seeing Deborah. "I heard no more screaming, and I feared the worst, that—"

He cut himself off when he saw Elisabeth's blood-drenched arms and saw the unmoving bundle in the basket.

"I'm afraid, Japheth, that the worst has happened. Our baby died in the womb."

Japheth closed his eyes and clenched his fists. "It's my fault. God is punishing me for my drinking."

"No, husband, no," Deborah said pleadingly, "do not blame yourself. It was my own rash words that caused this!"

Japheth looked as if he was about to respond, but before he could, Deborah heard a cry from the sitting room. "Father! Father!"

It was Hester, their third child. She came running into the bedroom. "Father, Mother, come quick!"

Elisabeth spoke sharply. "Your mother can come nowhere, quick or otherwise."

More gently, Deborah said, "Go with her, Japheth, see what it is." She said those words as much to get him to leave as to stop trying to claim responsibility for the child's death. In addition, the argument had fatigued her beyond her already considerable exhaustion.

Deborah heard the door open, then odd wailing sounds mixed in with the louder rain and thunder. After the door slammed shut, the storm's sounds subsided, but the wailing did not.

Moments later, Japheth came back, along with Hester, Joshua, and their fourth and fifth children, the twins Caleb and Moses. Junia, she knew, was keeping an eye on the littler children upstairs.

Japheth held some kind of tiny animal in his arms, and it was obviously the source of the wailing. It looked like a tiny lizard, but its sounds were very much like an infant in pain or anguish.

Deborah then noticed that blood oozed from the creature's side, and concern for the animal's wellbeing scrubbed away her tiredness, at least for the moment. "Elisabeth, some rags for Mr. Leeds, please."

"Right away, Mother Leeds." Elisabeth gathered what few rags she hadn't used for Deborah's birthing. A few she dipped into the pot of simmering water that was still over the fire, and then she brought both sets of rags over to Japheth. Between the two of them, they not only cleaned the creature's wound with the wet rags but also dried it off with those dry.

The creature's wailing lessened with being tended to, but it still sounded simply miserable.

Joshua said, "Hester saw it out on the patio, crying and bleeding."

"Can we keep it?" Hester asked. "Please?"

Deborah's garden was already home to a half-dozen cats and about ten chickens, so another mouth to feed in that regard was not an issue, assuming this thing ate whatever the other animals ate.

"The Lord would want us to care for the sick and injured," Caleb said.

Moses added, "It would be wrong to send it back out into the storm."

Japheth said, "I cannot argue with that."

"We will take care of it!" Caleb said.

And Moses put in, "We will feed it and love it and heal it of its horrible wound!"

But Deborah found herself casting a glance at the basket in the corner. Then she said, "Children, come here, quickly."

"Yes, Mother," they all said in near-perfect unison, and they walked over to face her.

Japheth hung back with Elisabeth, the former holding the creature while the latter made a bandage of one of the dry rags.

"I'm sorry to tell you, my children, that the sibling that we were to be blessed with today is not to be. The Lord has taken my child from me a-borning."

All four children's faces fell, and tears welled up in Hester's eyes. "I'm sorry, Mother."

"Joshua, I will need you to tell Junia and the other children for me, please. And Hester, you will need to take on many of my household duties until I am well enough to perform them."

"I will, Mother." Hester wiped her tears away and stuck out her chin to show that she was grown-up enough for this.

"Good. Now let us pray together for the soul of this poor child, taken from us far sooner than we would like." She reached out, and she and the children all joined their hands to hers.

They closed their eyes, and each prayed silently. For her part, Deborah prayed, not for the child's soul as she had requested of her children, but instead for forgiveness for her own sin of anger.

Several weeks passed, and eventually, Deborah was well enough to move around. Cousin Elisabeth had worked herself into exhaustion to take care of Deborah. By the time Deborah was recovered, Elisabeth had taken to bed with a horrible illness. Since Hester was doing quite well with most of Deborah's usual work around the house—indeed, she was turning into a much better cook than Deborah herself—she allowed Hester to continue to do so while the mother of the house returned the favor by caring for Elisabeth.

Meantime, Caleb and Moses were as good as their word. They cared for the creature, changing its dressing, feeding it the same feed they gave the chickens, and making sure it got plenty of water.

It must have been good for it—whatever it was—as it continued to grow. When they had found it on their doorstep, it fit in Japheth's hands. Now, though, after the better part of a month, it was as big as Muriel, their three-year-old girl.

Deborah examined the creature's wound and saw that it was not only completely closed, but there was also no scarring. "Remarkable."

When the creature replied with a deep, sibilant, "Thank you," Deborah screamed and ran from the bedroom and downstairs.

Japheth was in the living room, and he rose from his daily reading of the Bible to see what was the matter. "Deborah?"

"It—it *spoke*!"

"What spoke?"

"The—the—the animal! From the night of—the night of the storm!" She had been unable to speak aloud of the stillbirth ever since they buried the infant corpse behind the garden. She barely had been able to even think about it.

"That's not possible."

Then Caleb and Moses came running down the stairs.

"Mother!" Caleb cried.

"Father!" Moses screamed.

And then, in unison, they said, "Our pet is talking!"

"The devil, you say." Japheth clutched his Bible to his chest and immediately went upstairs.

Deborah was more than happy to remain downstairs, but Caleb said, "Mother, come see!"

Moses added, "It's amazing!"

In truth, Deborah had thought she was going mad. She was still not completely recovered from her ordeal, and Elisabeth grew sicker by the day.

But if Caleb and Moses also heard the creature speak, then perhaps it wasn't her own feverish imagining.

Deborah went back upstairs and heard the low, hissing voice once again.

"—am grateful to you for your assistance."

"Who are you?" Japheth asked.

"I am me," the animal said, and his tone made it sound as if that was the most ridiculous question.

"Do you have a name?" Japheth asked again. Deborah noticed that he was still clutching onto his Bible for dear life.

"I—" The creature hesitated. "I do not know. My first memory is being brought in from the rain. I only know how to speak because I have listened to you for all this time."

The nameless, talking beast had started to grow wings, and over the next week, he went from being unable to fly to darting across the garden.

One time, the creature flew outside when Cassandra Dickinson came by to purchase some healing herbs.

"You must stay in the house," Deborah admonished the animal after Cassandra left.

But then, the following day, the five-year-old, Ambrose, climbed the maple tree. Deborah had told him not to, and Japheth had told him not to, and Joshua and Junia had also told him not to, and yet, every time he walked outside, he climbed the maple.

Just as he always did, Japheth went to climb after him.

However, before he got more than a yard, the branch on which Ambrose sat, giggling, broke with a mighty snap.

Deborah's heart leapt into her throat as she watched her son plummet to the ground. She wanted to turn away but could not stop staring agape as Ambrose fell.

And then she nearly fainted from shock as the creature came as if from nowhere and caught Ambrose in his scaly arms, flying from the upstairs window to the outside and then lowering himself and Ambrose gently to the ground.

Ambrose started to cry, and Deborah comforted him. But as she did so, she heard Japheth say, "Thank you."

"I owe you my life," the creature said, "the very least I may do is save that of one of yours."

She asked Japheth to call a family meeting after that. Deborah sat in the living room with Japheth and the six oldest of the children. Elisabeth was too ill to attend, and she, along with the younger children, were all resting upstairs.

"I've never seen such an animal before," Joshua said. "And I have seen many beasts of the field in my time at the farm."

"I have seen much more than you, my son," Japheth said gravely, "and I have seen nothing that even resembles what is upstairs right now."

"He's not a what!" Caleb cried out.

"He's a he!" Moses said.

"I fear it is a minion of the devil," Deborah said.

"Mother," Joshua said, "he saved Ambrose's life!"

"And the twins are correct," Junia added. "He is not an 'it.' He speaks quite eloquently."

"The devil spoke eloquently when he tempted Eve in the garden," Deborah said.

Hester quoted the First Book of Peter: "'The devil prowls around like a roaring lion looking for someone to devour.'"

"He's not a lion!" Caleb yelled.

Japheth said, "He has been here a month, Deborah. If he meant us harm, would he not have done so? If he was a creature of Satan, would he have saved Ambrose's life?"

Deborah found herself unable to answer. She was convinced that the monster was sent to them as punishment for allowing their thirteenth son to die.

"There are no others of his kind that we know of," Japheth said. "And he has no memory of his life before. Can we really turn him out into the world where he will likely be attacked and beaten?"

"You don't know that," Deborah said weakly.

"When he spoke, you screamed," Japheth said. "And had he not been injured that night, would you have cowered in fear from him?"

"Perhaps." Deborah looked away in shame, for she knew that the people of the town would respond thusly, especially to the beast as he now was, the size of a small child. And why? Because of how he looked?

This time it was Joshua who quoted scripture. "'A righteous man has regard for the life of his beast.' Is he not our beast?"

Deborah found herself reminded of another Bible verse: the Lord Himself said in the Book of Psalms: "For every beast of the forest is Mine."

How could she be so cruel as to turn away one of God's creatures? Even if it was a strange one...

"We should name him," Caleb said.

Moses nodded. "I say we call him Moses!"

Unable to help herself, Deborah laughed. "And how will we tell the two of you apart?"

Junia said, "He is both the first of his kind and also the thirteenth child of this house. We should name him Unus Tredecim."

Deborah smiled. "That is a good name."

"But we should ask him if he will take it," Japheth said.

"Let's ask him!" Caleb said.

He ran upstairs, Moses trailing behind. Deborah smiled at Japheth, and they walked upstairs together.

By the time they made it to the bedroom where the creature was waiting, the twins had already breathlessly asked if he wished to be called "Unus Tredecim."

"I like the sound of that," he said. And for the first time, Deborah saw the creature's mouth widen in what she supposed was a smile.

No, not "the creature." Unus.

Deborah then looked at her husband. "'The wolf shall dwell with the lamb, and the leopard shall lie down with the young goat, and the calf and the lion and the fattened calf together; and a little child shall lead them.' Or, in our case, two little children."

"We're not little!" Moses said indignantly.

Elisabeth died the next day. The fever claimed her at last.

Her body was laid to rest in the Burying Ground, and they held a Meeting to honor her life.

Deborah spoke of how well Elisabeth served her as midwife for all twelve of her children. This caused a minor stir among the Friends, as everyone knew that she had had a thirteenth pregnancy, but nobody had heard anything about the outcome, and here she was obviously *not* pregnant.

Japheth closed the Meeting by quoting the Book of Matthew: "'Come to me, all who labor and are heavy laden, and I will give you rest. Take my yoke upon you and learn from me, for I am gentle and lowly in heart, and you will find rest for your souls. For my yoke is easy, and my burden is light.'"

A week after that Meeting, Junia was sitting with Margery, the pair of them working on a quilt for the Wigham family. Lucretia Nayler came in to inquire after the commission she had made for her daughter's dress.

"We're waiting for the dye to set," Margery said. "Tomorrow?"

"That is good to know, thank you." Lucretia shook her head and *tsk*ed. "That girl grows so fast, I'm like to need another dress from you in a month. As I'm here, do you know where I can find a remedy for an upset stomach? Both my sons have complained."

"Mother Leeds usually has the best—" Margery started, but Lucretia cut her off.

"Not *that* woman. She consorts with demons, she does."

Junia bridled but said nothing, as she was only the apprentice and still a child, and it was not her place to contradict an adult, especially one who was also a customer. But still, for Lucretia to say such things about Junia's family infuriated her.

To Junia's relief, Margery spoke on the Leeds' behalf. "Where on Earth did you get such a notion?"

"We were never told by the family about what happened to her most recent child. I heard she gave birth to a demon and that it then killed poor Elisabeth."

"I've never heard such nonsense," Margery said.

Unable to help herself, Junia said, "She did *not* give birth to a demon! My brother was dead in the womb!"

Lucretia looked stunned and confused, and Margery said, "My apprentice is Miss Junia Leeds."

Tsking again, Lucretia said, "Well, it's good that you're apprenticing to Mrs. Savery, then. Gets you out of that house of demons."

With that, she turned and left.

"I'm sorry about that," Margery said gently, putting a hand on Junia's.

"Thank you," Junia whispered. She shook with anger and nearly stabbed herself with the quilting needle.

A few days after that, Joshua brought berries to the Fothergill farmhouse in a wheelbarrow when he overheard two men talking on the front porch. He recognized one voice as Constantine Fothergill, the owner of the farm; the other voice was a stranger.

The stranger was speaking. "Old Emmett Kilworth swears he saw a devil with wings flying over the coastline."

"As I recall," Constantine said, "Emmett partakes of the contents of his wine barrels a bit too much."

"Maybe so, but he was with John Fisher, and he said the same. What's more, John swears he saw the same devil flying over the Leeds home."

Unus was helping Deborah and Hester prepare dinner when someone knocked on the front door.

Japheth had actually managed to find work, so Deborah called out to the twins to answer the door.

"We're going!" Caleb cried out as he and Moses ran down the stairs.

Deborah regarded Unus. "I'm sorry."

She said that every time someone visited. Unus had given up telling her that she had nothing to apologize for but instead flew out of the kitchen and into the living room, flying directly into the fireplace and up the chimney to hide until the visitor left.

It was young Levi Blackborow. The twins led him into the kitchen.

"I'm sorry to bother you, Mother Leeds," Levi said, "but Mater needs more of your willow bark for her headaches."

Deborah had always thought it endearing that the Blackborow children all called their parents "Mater" and "Pater." "Caleb, Moses, please help young Levi?"

"Yes, Mother," they both said in unison.

Even as the twins ran off to fetch the willow bark, Levi turned, then hesitated, and turned back around. "Also, Mother Leeds? Is everything well with you and yours?"

"My husband and oldest son are both working, and we are all hale and healthy. Why?"

"Then why have you spread a circle of salt around your house?"

Deborah felt her face fall into a scowl. It was apparently a particularly murderous expression, as Levi actually flinched. "We did no such thing!"

Hester asked, "Who would do that?"

When the twins returned with the willow bark, Deborah said, "Caleb, Moses, some fool has spread a circle of salt around our house. After you see young Levi out, please see to clearing it away?"

Again, they both spoke in unison: "Yes, Mother."

That winter, on the night of a terrible blizzard, Unus insisted on going out.

Deborah tried to talk him out of it. "How many times have you ventured out of this house? And still, you have found no others of your kind."

"I cannot give up, Mother," Unus said. "I cannot be the only one. There *must* be others. And with this snowfall, I am unlikely to be seen by prying eyes."

Wryly, Deborah said, "Prying eyes are determined to see you whether or not you leave the house."

"Indeed. I will return soon."

"Soon" turned out to be at the crack of dawn, as Unus returned to the house with a bundle cradled in his scaly arms.

Rubbing the sleep from her eyes, Deborah climbed out of bed and put a housecoat on over her nightclothes to fend off the winter cold. "Is that another of your kind?"

"No." Unus cradled the bundle in one arm while using his other taloned hand to brush the prodigious amounts of snow off his person.

Once that was done, he unwrapped the blanket to reveal a tiny animal that looked very much like a baby alligator, but instead of four short legs, it had two medium-sized legs and two longer arms with elbows and with fingers at the end, complete with thumbs.

"What is it?" Deborah asked.

Before Unus could speak, the creature muttered, "*Verlaten. Helpen. Ik smeek. Verlaten.*"

Unus then said, "I know not what it is, but it was very obviously in agony."

"More obviously than you know," Deborah said. "It's speaking Dutch." There were still many folk from the original Dutch settlers of this colony in the area, and while Deborah could not speak their tongue fluently, she knew enough to know that the creature was begging for help and had been abandoned.

She could no more turn her back on this one of God's creatures than she could Unus.

Like Unus, the tiny creature grew, though not as quickly. Deborah had named her Noortje, a Dutch name meaning "compassion." Like Unus, she stayed hidden when people came by, which was happening with less frequency as the stories about the Leeds family spread.

Unus never found another like himself, but he did find other creatures. Many were awful and wished harm upon Unus and upon other people. In particular, he came home one night in 1737 with a wound that was almost as vicious as the one he'd been afflicted with when he was on the Leeds doorstep that fateful stormy night. While Deborah and Hester tended to the wound, he told them of a being who walked like a man but had the face of a lizard. That being attacked Unus, leaving this wound, though Unus gave as good as he got.

But there were others he wished to rescue, and Deborah found she could not turn away any of them with a clear conscience.

Some only stayed for a few days, like the sasquatch that was trying to escape to the south, having been menaced in the French territories to the north, or the sea monster that had been wounded by a harpoon. Unus had nursed her back to health and then returned her to the ocean.

Another was a mute man-ape who seemed to speak in gestures, whom Unus had found in the Pine Barrens in 1739. Nootje had managed to find a way to communicate with him, and she started calling him Stomme. Hester also learned Stomme's gestural language, but Deborah found it beyond her.

By 1740, Caleb and Moses had joined Joshua at the Fothergill farm, and Junia was living with Margery as her assistant seamstress. Japheth was once again out of work, as the towns' stories about the Leeds family had grown more and more outlandish— but also gained more and more traction, which meant fewer and fewer people came to Deborah for herbal remedies or would hire Japheth, though he hadn't touched alcohol in years.

And, of course, those stories had at least some basis in truth.

But Deborah would not, *could* not turn away any of God's creatures who were in need of sanctuary. To do otherwise would violate everything the Society of Friends believed in.

And yet, their fellow Quakers thought of them as consorting with demons. But those that their foolish neighbors would call demons were in truth fine and noble folk. Unus, Nootje, and Stomme were as much part of the family as Deborah's dozen children.

A month previous, Unus had started laying eggs. Deborah had never seen anything like it, though her knowledge of animal husbandry was limited. However, Joshua — who was far more experienced in these matters — found it baffling as well, especially since the eggs didn't hatch.

With, eventually, one exception. A small creature, a doppelgänger to what Unus looked like that rainy night five years earlier, broke through one egg's shell. Unus named her Duo Tredecim.

Something would need to be done about the situation soon. The coin Joshua, Junia, Caleb, and Moses made was not enough to support the entire family, plus it wouldn't be long before Joshua and Junia would marry, thus adding even more mouths beyond Duo to the family in need of feeding.

A voice bellowed from outside the house, then: "Japheth and Deborah Leeds!"

After a moment, Deborah recognized the voice.

She went to the front window, and Japheth joined her from the back door, having just returned from the privy. "Is that Elder Ashbridge?"

"It is." Deborah pulled the curtain back to see the stooped-over, white-haired form of Cuthbert Ashbridge, the Elder of the Meeting in the town, standing with a crowd of their neighbors. Elder Ashbridge was holding a Bible in the air, his deep voice echoing throughout the garden.

"We beseech you to cast Satan out from your lives! You lie with the beasts, and they must be expunged, lest ye give in to wickedness! 'You shall not suffer a witch to live. Whoever lies with a beast shall surely be put to death!'"

Even as the elder quoted the Book of Exodus, two boys spread salt in a circle around the house.

"Begone, ye foul demons!" Elder Ashbridge cried.

Japheth stormed to the door.

Deborah reached out to him. "No, Japheth, don't! He's the elder!"

"I don't care if he's the second coming of the Lord Jesus Christ, I will not have him accusing me of such things!"

Shaking her head, Deborah considered and then followed her husband out the door. She would not let him take this stand alone.

"What do you think you're doing, Elder?" Japheth asked.

"Trying to save you, Japheth!" Elder Ashbridge held up his Bible. "'You shall love the Lord your God and serve Him with all your heart and soul.' You have strayed from the path of love for God, and you must find your way back!"

"We've never lost our way," Japheth said.

"Of course, you have! Your thirteenth child was transformed into a winged beast! It killed your midwife and has been menacing the township lo, these five years! It must be driven out!"

Deborah scoffed. "Are we papists now, casting exorcisms? There is no one here but our family. And there is nothing out there with you, save for people's foolish flights of fancy."

"Leave our home, Elder Ashbridge!" Japheth cried.

Shaking his wizened head, the elder lowered his arms, placing his Bible in his coat pocket with a heavy sigh. "We will all pray for you, my friends."

Slowly, the crowd dispersed, though the salt circle remained around the house.

Deborah took Japheth's hand, and the two of them reentered their home.

"What are we to do about this?" she asked as they walked across the threshold.

"It is obvious — we must depart."

Taken aback, Deborah saw that Unus, who had spoken, was standing in the living room with Nootje and Stomme.

Stomme was gesturing, and Nootje translated: "We are too much of a burden for you to bear. And I agree with him," she added, speaking for herself in her accented English. "You have been kind to us, Mother Leeds, Father Leeds — more than we deserve. But we must find our own path."

Unus added, "I wish to raise Duo in a place where she may roam freely."

Japheth winced. "I fear no such place exists."

"In fact, we have already found such a place," Nootje said with a sharp-toothed smile. "It is deep in the Pine Barrens, far from prying eyes. We would only ask your help, Father Leeds."

"How so?" Japheth asked.

Unus said, "We wish to construct a home, but we have no skills in carpentry."

Japheth smiled. "It would be my honor to teach you those skills and help you build a house."

Chapter Four

The Pine Barrens
State of New Jersey, United States of America
January 1909

Quinque Tredecim gestured to the house they all sat in. "This is the home that Japheth Leeds built for my great-great-grandfather."

Josiah Clevenger listened in abject shock. He had heard many tales of the Leeds Devil since becoming a Slayer, and some aspects of Quinque's story matched details of those stories.

But this was far more than he had expected from his search for the Jersey Devil.

Quinque continued: "From the moment that my great-great-grandfather, alongside my infant great grandmother, Stomme, and Nootje crossed the threshold of this house, it became a sanctuary for those whom the human world views as monsters, but who do not deserve such an appellation."

The jackalope spoke for the first time, the creature having a very high, very squeaky voice. "I came here seeking sanctuary alongside a gumberoo, but when Quattuor learned that the gumberoo had killed a man, he was turned away."

Quinque had been pacing back and forth in front of the fireplace while telling her story, but now she stopped and regarded Josiah with a penetrating stare. "We have taken a grave risk this day, Mr. Clevenger. Our fates — all of our fates — are in your hands. This sanctuary has stood for one hundred and sixty-nine years. It is within your power to either allow us to continue to do our good work for the innocents under our roof or destroy it and us forever."

Josiah turned away from the Jersey Devil's intense stare and instead focused his gaze upon the fire that roared in front of him.

He thought about the $10,000 — possibly $20,000 — he could get from the Philadelphia Zoo if he turned in the Tredecims to them.

He thought about the fact that neither Quinque nor Quattuor had actually harmed anyone.

He thought about his commission from Grimwade, which was only that the Jersey Devil be "dealt with."

He thought about how any one of the creatures in this house could easily kill him, and if they all acted in concert, Josiah would have absolutely no chance of survival. That they didn't do so, but instead offered him hospitality, bespoke their sincerity.

And finally, he thought about the words Miss Silverio spoke to him back in Camden: *"Are we not people of reason who may talk and find a solution?"*

He had told Miss Silverio that his function as a Slayer was to kill the creatures of the devil that he was hired to hunt. In fact, his words to her were appallingly similar to the words spoken to the Leeds family by Elder Ashbridge in the 18th century. As Quinque had told the tale, Josiah had thought the old Quaker to be a small-minded fool. Yet how could he condemn that long-dead gentleman when Josiah himself had felt the same way?

Finally, he looked back at Quinque. "I propose an arrangement, Miss Tredecim."

Quinque folded her arms. "And what would that be, Mr. Clevenger?"

"If you keep your word that you will remain here in the Pine Barrens and no longer menace the people of the Delaware Valley, then I will say that I drove you off and keep the secret of this place. What's more, I will keep an eye out for others who may require your sanctuary and lead them to you."

The lizard man hissed, his tongue flicking out of his mouth. "Why should we trust your word?"

"I left my weapon outside this house, sir," Josiah said, and the lizard man was visibly taken aback by the respect Josiah showed him with the salutation of "sir." "Further, the alternative to taking me at my word is to do me harm, and I do not believe you will do that for two reasons." He enumerated the reasons on his fingers. "First, it would belie my host's insistence that you only would commit violence for defensive purposes. I am an unarmed man who is enjoying your hospitality. There is nothing I have done or am doing against which you need to defend. And second, I was hired by the Campbell Soup Company, one of the largest industries in the region. Rest assured, if I disappear without a trace, they will simply hire someone else."

In fact, Josiah was not at all sure that his second point was true. Campbell Soup only hired a Slayer because of the extreme circumstance, and it was Josiah they hired because of Grimwade's prior knowledge of him. There was no guarantee that they would seek out another Slayer following his hypothetical disappearance.

Sokanon spoke up, then. "Whatever I may think of this Slayer and his kind, I will say that he treated me with respect when he captured and returned me to the Tribal Council. I believe we can take him at his word."

"Thank you." Josiah said those two words with as much feeling as he could muster, for he knew that the Thunderbird did not speak well of someone without cause.

Quinque unfolded her arms, spit on her right hand, and then held it out. "I believe the custom is to clasp hands in this manner to seal a bargain."

Josiah stood up, spit on his right hand, and clasped hers. It felt like gripping a boot, but it was, nonetheless, a handshake.

"I must return to Camden and inform my client that his commission has been fulfilled." He hesitated and gave Quinque a sidelong glance. "I would, ah, prefer not to return via the method by which I arrived."

Saltadora let out a braying laugh. "That won't be necessary! I will drive you!"

It was late at night by the time Josiah was returned to Camden. The giant monkey Saltadora had in his possession a Sharp

Speedster, an automobile manufactured in Trenton. The ride was slow and difficult, particularly in the Pine Barrens themselves, but things sped up considerably once they were on proper cobblestone roads.

Saltadora had dressed in a large coat, an oversized hat, and a scarf across his face, as well as thick gloves to hide his true nature. The chill weather aided in the deception, as nobody questioned someone so well-bundled. Indeed, Josiah found himself missing his hat as they drove through the winter night.

When Saltadora brought the Speedster to a halt in front of Mrs. Van Leuwen's boarding house, Josiah turned to the simian and said, "Thank you, sir."

"You need not thank me, Mr. Clevenger. You are doing us a great service. I hope that you will continue to provide it."

"For as long as the Tredecims' rule that none who live within your walls have done any harm is obeyed, I will indeed do so." He offered a hand.

Saltadora stared at it in what was probably surprise — it was difficult to judge with his entire face covered — and then returned it. He had an awkward but strong grip.

Josiah entered the boarding house and went straight upstairs to his room. The excitement of the day, the fascination of the story of the Jersey Devil, and the novelty of the automobile ride all fell away like leaves in autumn, leaving only sheer exhaustion behind. Josiah collapsed on his bed without even removing his clothing or the Horvath amulet.

As ever, he woke up at dawn and had a hearty breakfast and more talk of the Jersey Devil with Mrs. Van Leuwen. Josiah continued to express his skepticism regarding the creature's existence, a fiction that proved easier to maintain than expected, as the reality of the Jersey Devil was extremely far removed from the rumors and tall tales that had spread through the region over the past week.

He was not surprised to find Oliver had already opened the store, as he had not sent word that he was done with his work as a Slayer.

He was, however, completely surprised to discover Mr. Grimwade already waiting for him.

As Josiah entered, Oliver said, "Good morning, Jed. This gentleman is here to see you. Says he's your client."

"He is," Josiah said, removing his coat and scarf, reaching for his hat, and then snapping his fingers with disappointment as he remembered that it was gone forever. He really did love that hat.

Grimwade had a wide smile. "I wanted to congratulate you on a job well done, Mr. Clevenger."

That brought Josiah up short. "Word travels fast," he said slowly. "I was going to venture to the factory this morning to inform you."

"No need." Grimwade held up his left hand, in which he held a rolled-up piece of paper. He unrolled it to reveal a poster from the Arch Museum in Philadelphia. "These signs are all over Philadelphia and Camden, at least, according to my associates."

Grimwade held the poster up high for closer examination. Josiah saw that it included a drawing of the Leeds Devil that looked less like Quinque and Quattuor than Speelman's sketch had—the wings were too big, the tail too long, the legs too straight. The poster's headline read, "CAUGHT!!! AND HERE!!! ALIVE!!! THE LEEDS DEVIL, Captured Friday After a Terrific Struggle."

"I'm surprised," Grimwade was saying, "that you turned it in to the museum rather than the zoo since the latter was offering a reward."

Josiah hesitated. "I thought it would not be in keeping with the spirit of our arrangement if I took further remuneration for my efforts," he finally said.

"Very considerate of you, sir. Nonetheless, on behalf of Mr. Campbell, Mr. Speelman, and the rest of Joseph Campbell and Company, I thank you for your efforts." He rolled up the poster and pulled a check out of his coat pocket. "Here is a bank check that should cover the balance of your fee. Please feel free to invoice my office for the expenses."

Taking the check, Josiah said, "Thank you."

"No, sir, thank *you*. You have done a great service this day."

With that, Grimwade took his leave.

Josiah looked down at the check. It wasn't enough to remodel the store. But it was enough to pay him for his time. After all, he did deal with the Jersey Devil as asked. He had no idea what it was that the Arch Museum had on display, but if it helped sell the notion that he had stopped the Jersey Devil's rampage, he would take it.

He looked at Oliver. "I'm going to deposit this check in the bank, and then I will take over the store. Thank you for helping us, Ollie."

"My pleasure, Jed."

Josiah put his coat and scarf back on and headed toward the bank. He was looking forward to a day of nothing more than selling dry goods and dealing with customers — even if they were likely to still be gossiping about the Leeds Devil. He would listen to their stories and nod and smile and be secure in the knowledge that he knew the truth and that Quinque, Quattuor, and the others should remain safe in the Pine Barrens.

Chapter Five

By the time Valentina Perrone finished telling Sarah el-Guindi the story of the Tredecim family of Jersey Devils, she was pulling the Equinox into the parking lot adjacent to the Atlantic Resorts Casino and Hotel.

"So Unus was male," Sarah was saying, "but he laid eggs?"

"Yup." Having taken a ticket from the machine as she entered the lot, Valentina was now driving up the ramp in search of a spot. Despite it being the off-season, most of the spots were still taken. "Every generation, one suddenly lays a whole bunch of eggs, no matter what gender they identify as, and then one of them hatches. And only one, and after that, they don't lay no more. Duo grew up and laid an egg that hatched, and that was Tribus. Tribus laid an egg, which grew up to be Quattuor."

"And Quattuor's no longer alive?"

Finally finding an empty space between a Toyota Corolla and a Chevrolet Colorado pickup truck, Valentina turned into the spot. "Nah, he died about a month after that mess in 1909."

"So that wasn't him on display at the Arch Museum?"

Valentina laughed as she turned the ignition off. "Nah, that was a kangaroo that they painted a stripe on and glued a couple of wings to."

"So it had nothing to do with Josiah Clevenger?"

"Kinda?" Valentina got out of the Equinox, as did Sarah, then walked around to the back to open the rear hatch. "So that cab driver that took him down to Chester, his brother worked for the Arch Museum, so that's how that happened."

"That means that Clevenger was at least partly responsible for the exhibit?"

"Partly, yeah." Valentina grabbed a Beauvoir charm from the case in the trunk, as well as a bag of Swedish Fish, and a large blanket.

Sarah stared at what Valentina was holding as she pushed the button that closed the rear hatch. "That's a charm that can remove all the moisture from the air—I can't remember the name now."

"Beauvoir," Valentina said.

"Right! Magickal items are named for the person who first created the spell that the item utilizes."

The garage had three exits on each floor, one that led to the street, one that led to the casino/hotel, and one that led to the boardwalk. Valentina walked toward the latter since they needed to search the beach.

Sarah continued as they walked through the boardwalk exit, which took them to a covered outdoor staircase. "Which begs the question—Swedish Fish?"

"Etienne loves them."

"And you happened to have some in the car?"

"Not 'happened,' I *also* love them. I always keep a bunch in the car."

"Why in the trunk? That makes them harder to get at."

"'Cause it makes them harder to get at. I don't need *more* junk food in my life, thanks."

They walked out onto the wooden slats of the boardwalk, which was sparsely populated on this cold February afternoon. Not empty by any means, but at this same time, on a weekday afternoon in warmer weather, it would be wall-to-wall people.

The area directly behind the hotel was an extended pier with a restaurant, so Valentina walked further down the boardwalk to where she could see the beach. Shivering, she zipped up her down coat—it was about five degrees colder here than it had been in the Pine Barrens, and the wind whipped in off the ocean.

A short man with long hair blowing in his face was talking on a smartphone while leaning against the fence that separated the boardwalk from the beach. He ended his call, put his phone in his pocket, and then his eyes went wide, and he screamed: "What the hell's *that*?"

Valentina followed the man's gaze and saw a green figure swimming in the ocean, diving into the waves that broke on the sand. It was certainly the right skin tone to be Etienne, but she couldn't tell from this far out, and with him only occasionally peeking out from underwater.

Muttering, "I am *not* wearing the right shoes for this," Valentina ran over to the nearest staircase that led to the beach.

Sarah lagged behind and said something to the person who'd seen Etienne.

Valentina hated walking on sand. Always had, ever since she was a little girl. Her parents would take her down the Shore, and she'd stumble and fall down as soon as they got to the beach.

At least she didn't fall down this time, despite wearing boots that were great for walking on sidewalks that were covered in a mix of salt, snow, and ice, but not so hot for sand. Plus, her dark hair kept blowing into her face when the wind shifted, and she only had her right hand to shove her hair out of her eyes as the blanket was under her left arm.

Once she was close to the shore, she cried out, "Etienne!"

Suddenly, a green-skinned head poked out from the water with a face like that of a fish. "*Qu'est-ce que?* Val?"

"What the hell are you doing, Etienne?"

"Swimming! Is it not wonderful? I love to swim!"

"Yeah, I know that, Etienne, but people can see you."

"What do you mean? It is winter! There are no people on the boardwalk in..." He trailed off, as he had looked past Valentina at the boardwalk as he was talking. "Those are people."

"Yeah, Etienne. Not a lot of people, but there are some. And they've got phones with cameras. Now c'mon, Quinque and the others are worried about you."

"They are? Even Walter?"

Valentina chuckled. "Okay, maybe not Walter, but the rest of them are. Now, let's get you home before you scare more people."

Etienne waded out toward her, his webbed hands waving back and forth while his legs pushed through the waves as they receded.

"I do not wish to scare people, Val. I only wish to swim."

"I know, Etienne." Valentina unfolded the blanket and wrapped it around Etienne's dark green, scaly form. "C'mon. I've got some Swedish Fish with me."

"*Très bien!*"

The blanket covered enough of Etienne that not too many people noticed that there was a mugwump in their midst.

Sarah was still at the top of the stairs, her hijab keeping her hair from blowing in her face, which marked the first time Valentina had been envious of the religious doctrine that dictated that Sarah wear it.

"Etienne, this is my apprentice, Sarah el-Guindi."

"Hello, Etienne," she said.

"*Bonjour*, Sarah," Etienne said.

"What did you tell that guy?" Valentina asked Sarah.

"I convinced him not to call the police—I said it was a family member who likes to play dress-up. I *believe* he bought it. In case he did not, however—"

"We're gonna head out. C'mon, Etienne." Valentina reached into her coat pocket and pulled out the Swedish Fish. Etienne's recessed eyes seemed to light up at the sight.

She gave him the bag, which he struggled to open with his wet, webbed hands.

Pulling out her smartphone, Valentina said to Sarah, "Help him out, would you please?"

As the three of them walked toward the entrance to the parking lot, Valentina called Rocco.

After three rings: "Amalfitano."

"Rocco, it's Valentina. I got your beach monster, and I'm taking it somewhere safe."

"Thank Christ, I just got another tourist bitching about it. And in less than twenty-four hours, too. Nice work, Val."

"We aim to please. I'll e-mail you an invoice tonight."

"Great. Thanks."

Valentina smiled as they started up the covered staircase to the parking garage. Always nice when it was an easy job that paid well.

An hour later, they pulled back next to the station wagon in front of the wooden house in the middle of the Pine Barrens. This time, Quinque—no longer wearing an apron—and Jimmy the mothman both came out the front door as the car approached.

"Etienne, you had us worried," Quinque said without preamble.

"*Je suis desolé*, Quinque."

Jimmy then let loose with some rapid-fire French that Valentina could not follow, and Etienne responded in kind.

Etienne and Jimmy went inside, continuing their argument in French, while Quinque approached Valentina and Sarah. "Thank you, Ms. Perrone. I am grateful that Coursers have continued to aid us rather than attack us."

"I meant to ask about that," Sarah said. "Josiah Clevenger was the only Courser—or Slayer, whatever—who knew about your home. How do so many know now?"

"Word got out over the years," Quinque said, "and Mr. Clevenger was forced to expand the circle of knowledge. But it has remained a closely guarded secret. Now then, I know I offered you leftover chicken soup, but may I ask that you stay for supper? Ms. el-Guindi, you will be happy to know that I have prepared a meat-less dish for you."

Sarah seemed utterly baffled. "I'm sorry?"

"You said you did not consume meat. Therefore, I have prepared a meal for you with no meat."

Valentina grinned at her apprentice. "Guess we're staying for dinner, huh?"

"I guess we are." Sarah shook her head ruefully, and the three of them entered the house.

The living room was much emptier than it had been before, as only Jimmy and Etienne were there, still arguing in French.

Looking to the right, Valentina saw that everyone else was gathered around the large dining room table. There were five more place settings than there were folks seated at the table; one of those was the head of the table, which was, naturally, reserved for Quinque. Valentina noted that it was almost a full house, with only Izzy and Nguyet missing. Izzy was too big to fit at the table, and mokele-mbembes only ate twice a week, in any case, and nobody could stand to watch Nugyet eat, so the giant spider took his meals in the attic.

"Etienne, James, it's time for supper," Quinque said, and the mugwump and the mothman both nodded and took two of the empty seats. Sarah and Valentina slid into the remaining two, leaving the head of the table for the Jersey Devil.

"So," Valentina asked Sarah as she sat down next to Walter the sasquatch and across from a primate that just had to be Munish, "what do you think of this halfway house for monsters?"

Sarah looked around the table occupied by nine different strange creatures. "Halfway house? With all the many and varied beings who've lived here over the centuries, this is more like an all-the-way house."

Acknowledgments

All-the-Way House pulls liberally from numerous different tales of the Jersey Devil, as well those of the other cryptids that appear herein. Many of the characters in the 1909 and 1735 portions of the novella are based on people from those tales. Likewise, several of the journalistic accounts mentioned in the story are from actual newspapers of the time.

The following sources were invaluable: *The Ancient and Esoteric Order of the Jackalope, Ancient Origins*, the Atlantic County web site, the *Digest* ezine, *Enchiridion*, the *Philadelphia Inquirer*, and *Weird New Jersey*.

Thanks to Danielle Ackley-McPhail, Mike McPhail, and Greg Schauer of eSpec Books, as well as all the fine folks at Cryptid Crate, for inviting me to play in this particular sandbox.

Thanks to all the usual suspects: my in-house editors GraceAnne Andreassi DeCandido and Wrenn Simms, as well as nearest and dearest, ToniAnn Marini, Meredith Peruzzi, the Forebearance, the folks at the dojo, plus Matthew, Kyle, Anneliese, Sas, and of course, Kaylee, Louie, Spot, Hima, Professor Zoom, Loki, Thor, Tempura, and Jazz. Thanks also to New Jersey and Philadelphia area locals Joseph Berenato, Hugh Casey, Helena Frank, Gregory Frost, Ian Hanley, Jonathan Maberry, and Zan Rosin, as well as to the late great Doris Dehnert Peters, who financed all those trips to Atlantic City over the years.

eSpec Books Titles by
Keith R.A. DeCandido

Dragon Precinct
Unicorn Precinct
Goblin Precinct
Gryphon Precinct
Mermaid Precinct
Tales from Dragon Precinct
(forthcoming)
Phoenix Precinct
Manticore Precinct
More Tales from Dragon Precinct
Without A License

(co-written with David Sherman)
To Hell and Regroup
The 18th Race Omnibus

eSpec Books Titles including
Keith R.A. DeCandido

The Best of Bad-Ass Faeries
The Best of Defending the Future
Footprints in the Stars
Devilish and Divine

Keith R.A. DeCandido has written several other tales of Coursers (or Slayers) and their work keeping the world safe from supernatural threats, including the novels *A Furnace Sealed* and the forthcoming *Feat of Clay* (both from WordFire Press) and the short stories "Under the King's Bridge" in *Liar Liar* (Mendacity Press), "Materfamilias" in *Bad Ass Moms* (Crazy 8 Press), and "Unguarded" in *Devilish and Divine* (eSpec Books).

His other work includes media tie-in fiction in more than thirty different licensed universes from *Alien* to *Zorro*, as well as fiction in his own worlds, including fantastical police procedurals in the fictional cities of Cliff's End and Super City, as well as urban fantasy tales in the somewhat real locales of Key West and New York City. He also writes pop-culture commentary, primarily for the award-winning site Tor.com, but also for various books and magazines.

Recent and upcoming work includes the novels *Phoenix Precinct* (the next in his series of police procedurals in an epic fantasy setting, from eSpec Books), *Animal* (a thriller written with Dr. Munish K. Batra, from WordFire), *To Hell and Regroup* (a military science fiction novel written with David Sherman, from eSpec Books), and the aforementioned *Feat of Clay*; short stories in the anthologies *Pangaea* Book 3: *Redemption* (Crazy 8), *Footprints in the Stars* (eSpec), *Across the Universe: Tales of Alternative Beatles* (Fantastic Books), and *Turning the Tied* (a charity anthology from the International Association of Media Tie-in Writers); and new graphic novels from TokyoPop in the world of *Resident Evil*, tying into the Netflix animated series *Infinite Darkness*.

Keith is also a third-degree black belt in karate (he both teaches and trains), a professional musician (currently percussionist for the parody band Boogie Knights), an editor of many years' standing (though he usually does it sitting down), and probably some other stuff he can't recall due to the lack of sleep. Find out less at his website at DeCandido.net.

artist's rendition of a Jersey Devil

THE JERSEY DEVIL

(Also known in folklore and the media as The Devil of Leeds, The Leeds Devil, Jabberwock, Woozle Bug, kangaroo horse, kingowing, flying death, flying horse, flying hoof, and cowbird.)

ORIGINS: Said to have been born the thirteenth child of the Leeds family in 1735, in the Pine Barrens of New Jersey.

After having already borne twelve children, Mother Leeds (Jane or Deborah, depending on the account) cursed having another when the family's situation was already precarious.

It is believed the father was Japheth or Daniel Leeds, or a British soldier who kept Mother Leeds as a mistress. Some even claim she was a witch and the babe's father the Devil.

Folklore says the child either was born a hairy creature at the offset, or born normal in all aspects, but swiftly transformed, flying up and away through the chimney. One account claims the child's transformation was the result of a gypsy curse. By any account, the Jersey Devil has been terrorizing the region ever since.

DESCRIPTION: The Jersey Devil's appearance has remained consistent in most accounts, where the creature is said to be a winged biped with a horse-like head, cloven hooves, clawed hands, and a tail. Interestingly enough, the hereditary Leeds family crest features a wyvern, a dragon-like creature with bat-like wings. As for the creature's voice, it is said to emit hissing, piercing shrieks, and terrible cries.

While these features remain generally the same, some reports cite slight variations, such as horns, a goat's head, snake's tail, forked tail, bat wings, or glowing (red) eyes.

There have also been wildly different accounts where the creature is humanoid with a deer or dog head, bird legs, or kangaroo-like body.

The reported height range spans from three and a half feet to the height of a man.

The creature is also believed to be impervious to harm, having been fired upon by guns and even artillery, without any effect.

LIFE CYCLE: According to folklore, the Jersey Devil was born human and cursed into its final form. There are no theories as to its reproduction or life span.

HISTORY: Starting in the early 18th century and continuing through the 20th century, there have been reports of the Jersey Devil everywhere from its native Pine Barrens, all over South Jersey, up toward Trenton, and even North Jersey and Pennsylvania.

After its purported birth, accounts of hoof prints and ravaged livestock, particularly chickens, were common in the area.

In 1740, traveling missionaries exorcised the Devil from the region for 100 years, but there were still reported sightings during that time.

Not much was documented until 1820, when Joseph Bonaparte (Napoleon's brother) was reported to have come face to face with the beast while hunting alone at his Bordentown estate.

In 1909, a rash of sightings sensationalized by the media led to what is called the Week of Terror, where Jersey Devil encounters were reported in not only in New Jersey, but Pennsylvania, Delaware and Maryland. Posses scoured the countryside, yelling "If you're the Jersey Devil, rattle your chains," but the dogs refused to follow the tracks. In both the countryside and the towns and cities, the Jersey Devil is said to have tormented citizens, attacking trolley cars, making off with livestock, and accosting people outside social clubs. It was bad enough that many people refused to leave their homes. Schools and other places of business closed. Ministers, however, noted an increase in attendance.

Sightings were more sparring after that notable week, but they still persist over the years, with reports of Jersey Devil tracks, corpses, and photographs feeding the legend.

There are no accounts of the Jersey Devil attacking humans, but he is considered a harbinger of doom, having been sited before every major war, and it is said he will perform acts of mischief against those who hold evil thoughts.

The Philadelphia Zoo even offered a $10,000 reward for the capture of the Jersey Devil, and the Arch Museum perpetuated one of the most famous hoaxes in a bid to save itself from closure, purchasing a kangaroo from a circus, which was then painted and false wings and claws attached. It was billed as a captured Jersey Devil, but the exhibit was not sufficient to save the museum.

Theory: Some propose that these legends stem from mass hysteria, other believe the Jersey Devil could actually be a living pterodactyl, trapped in the limestone caves, fed on subterranean fish and released by seismic activity.

ABOUT THE ARTIST

Although Jason Whitley has worn many creative hats, he is at heart a traditional illustrator and painter. With author James Chambers, Jason collaborates and illustrates the sometimes-prose, sometimes graphic novel, *The Midnight Hour,* which is being collected into one volume by eSpec Books. His and Scott Eckelaert's newspaper comic strip, Sea Urchins, has been collected into four volumes. Along with eSpec Books' Systema Paradoxa series, Jason is working on a crime noir graphic novel. His portrait of Charlotte Hawkins Brown is on display in the Charlotte Hawkins Brown Museum.

CAPTURE THE CRYPTIDS!

Cryptid Crate is a monthly subscription box filled with various cryptozoology- and paranormal-themed items to wear, display, and collect. Expect a carefully curated box filled with creeptastic pieces from indie makers and artisans pertaining to bigfoot, sasquatch, UFOs, ghosts, and other cryptid and mysterious creatures (apparel, decor, media, etc).

http://CryptidCrate.com